The White Glove War

KATIE CROUCH

AND GRADY HENDRIX

poppy

LITTLE, BROWN AND COMPANY
NEW YORK   BOSTON

Also by Katie Crouch

The Magnolia League
Men and Dogs
Girls in Trucks

Poppy
Hachette Book Group
237 Park Avenue, New York, NY 10017
For more of your favorite series and novels, visit our website at www.pickapoppy.com

Poppy is an imprint of Little, Brown and Company.
The Poppy name and logo are trademarks of Hachette Book Group, Inc.

First Edition: July 2012

Library of Congress Cataloging-in-Publication Data

Crouch, Katie.
The white glove war : a Magnolia League novel / by Katie Crouch and Grady Hendrix.— 1st ed.
p. cm.
Summary: Told in separate voices, Alex, Hayes, and other members of Savannah's Magnolia League seek aid for their own family members from the legendary hoodoo family the Buzzards, in violation of an old pact, unaware that a Shadow Man is using one of them to return from the dead.
ISBN 978-0-316-18750-3
[1. Debutantes—Fiction. 2. Voodooism—Fiction. 3. Spirits—Fiction. 4. Grandmothers—Fiction. 5. Social classes—Fiction. 6. Savannah (Ga.)—Fiction.]
I. Hendrix, Grady. II. Title.
PZ7.C88513Whi 2012
[Fic]—dc23   2011031864

10 9 8 7 6 5 4 3 2 1
RRD-C
Printed in the United States of America

For Amanda

THESE SECRETS AND CHARMS THAT BIND US

ARE MUCH TOO PRECIOUS FOR BREATH,

YET THE SILENT SHACKLES AROUND OUR HEARTS

WILL PROTECT US LONG AFTER DEATH.

— From the *Magnolia League Young Debutante's Handbook*,
penned and printed by Khaki Pettit,
September 1961

There is life and there is death, but on the border, where one shades into the other, there is the In Between. The opening is no bigger than your fingernail; most people go through life without even knowing it's there. When they die, their spirits flutter past for just a fraction of a second. Everyone who dies glimpses the place, but very few choose to stay.

He's been there longer than any of the others. Every day it's agony to hold on, and every hour he's tempted to just give up and die. Most spirits do. They can't bear the pain of the limbs and mind slowly numbing, and so they flee to the other side. If they could, they would return to life. But that, of course, is impossible.

Yet William Long doesn't believe that. He has vowed that he will return to the waking world, no matter what the cost. And so he clings to the un-life. He was already used to pain when he arrived, as they had sewn his eyes shut long before they hanged him, intent on depriving him of his sight in the After. He'd had the last laugh. William learned long ago he doesn't need his own eyes to see—he just uses the ones he steals.

And now someone has opened the door: a lady

with an evil spirit and a pretty young face. Her jealousy has given him a way back. Every day she makes offerings to him, and every day he gets stronger. Her initial requests were simple enough: *Take the girls*—a mother and daughter. William Long has finished one, and now he waits for the other. What his conjurer doesn't know is that once he gets the girl, he'll be strong enough to keep going all on his own.

But for now he just lingers near her, waiting for an opening. The dead are never in a hurry. So, as if enjoying a last, drawn-out supper, he sips on Alexandria's shadows. He hovers nearby, preparing to devour her dreams.

1

Hayes

My name is Hayes Mary McCord Anderson. I'm named after my great-grandmother, Hayes Mary McCord, and while you've probably never heard of her, in my house she's practically a celebrity. Not a day goes by when my grandmother doesn't say her name at least once.

"Big Hayes" was born in 1902, when Savannah was at its poorest and saddest, and she was "empowered" before anyone even knew what that meant.

Great-Great-Granddad was in shipping, and the family château on Gaston Street was super fancy, until the War of Northern Aggression came and General Sherman launched his cowardly attack on the city.

My family lost everything. But Big Hayes's mother was proud and resourceful, and she managed to save up enough money to send her little girl off to boarding school. By the time Big Hayes returned to Savannah, she had her education and her mother was dead of malaria. The first thing Big Hayes did was sell the house on Gaston Street and marry a distant cousin who had inherited so much land upstate that just selling it off was a full-time job. Next, she started the Savannah Society for Ladies, the Citizens League, and the Historical Preservation Core. When Yankee developers began tearing down old houses to put up parking lots, she put on her dungarees and lay down in the middle of Barnard Street to stop them from running a fire road through Pulaski Square.

There is, however, one thing about Big Hayes McCord that no one will tell you. It's one of our family secrets, hidden away under lock and key. You won't be able to find it out for yourself in any library or archive, either, because my grandmother has carefully and systematically destroyed every shred of evidence.

You see, Hayes Mary McCord, like many of the McCords before her, was not blessed with beauty. According to legend, she had pores the size and color

4

of oily raisins. Her fingers were like sausages, her hair the texture of a used diner mop. One eye was three times as big as the other, and her nose had a bump on the end as large as a plum. She was so hideous, my grandmother Sybil once confided to me, it was a miracle she married at all. If not for her truly sparkling personality, she would have been doomed. As it was, the distant cousin she married was blind in one eye, and the only thing he was passionate about was collecting beetles. And then they had Sybil.

"It's a miracle," my grandmother says, "that I turned out as pretty as I did."

Then she looks at both of us in the mirror as if she can hardly believe it herself.

"We could practically be sisters."

However, what my grandmother and my mother and I all know is that our beauty is no miracle. It is bought and paid for. In 1957, a deal was struck in the woods with a man named Doc Buzzard. I've benefited greatly from this deal, as have all my sisters in the Magnolia League. But the price—for all of us—has been very, very high.

It's a cool, beckoning morning. The drama of the holidays has taken a serious toll on my looks, and my charms are due for renewal soon, meaning that I have to be extra careful. I don't want to go outside looking like I'm unraveling, so before I go, I take a quick Brighten-Me Bath—herbs steeped in peppermint, frankincense, and a drop of wasp pollen—then apply a little Buzzard Eye Bright tincture to my inner lids and give my hair a good Sina-Ever-Shine Steam. A quick hop back and forth over a bundle of birch sticks to ensure my powers of natural attraction, plus a drop of hawk's blood behind the ear for resilience and wisdom, has me ready to face the day. These potions don't smell all that wonderful, but they're effective; by the time I'm done, the dog won't go near my bathroom, but I look and feel like a million dollars. Having put in enough beauty work to hold me over for the day, I go downstairs to put on my cashmere peacoat and then head to the sunporch to tell my mother I'm going out.

Though beautiful, our Pulaski Square house—which boasts five bedrooms, a drawing room, a dining room, a cupola, and a library—is fairly modest by Magnolia League standards. With the help of the Buzzards, none of us ever have financial difficulties, and most of the Leaguers believe that the size of your house should reflect the size of your bank account. My father, Claude, added the cupola in a last-ditch attempt to make a peace offering to my grandmother. She had always complained that our house didn't have a profile that was "significant enough," whatever that means. But Dad's plan didn't work, the fighting continued, and pretty soon he went off to Paris. Actually, I don't know for sure that Paris is where he ended up. He didn't tell my mother where he was going when he left, but in my heart I know it's France. But then, I'm sort of obsessed with all things French.

"Absolutely not," I hear my grandmother saying as I approach the sunporch. "Three marriages should be enough for any woman." I freeze in place. I didn't know Grandmother was here. If she sees me, I'm not getting out of here for at least an hour. She's going to want to go over what I must—and what I absolutely *mustn't*—do at the meeting this afternoon. I start to quietly back away.

"But Booker's so dull," my mother complains. "He's driving me crazy."

Not that I'm a part of the conversation, but for the record let me just say that my stepfather isn't dull. He's dependable. There is a difference.

"All husbands are dull," my grandmother says. "Part of a wife's job is to pretend they're not. You absolutely may not get another divorce. Think of the family."

"*Claude* was never dull," my mother says, and I hear a clink of glass on glass as she pours herself another drink. Probably something alcoholic.

"Claude was worse than dull," my grandmother says. "Claude was *not suitable*. And if you hadn't had your head full of Harlequin Romances, you would have instantly realized that."

"Mother, if I hadn't met Claude, I wouldn't have had those beautiful children."

"Cuts both ways, Ellie. The children are saints and blessings, but if you hadn't met him, then I wouldn't have had to *take steps*. Haaaaaaayes!"

My heart flutters, but I recover quickly and make sounds on the steps as if descending, then clatter through the parlor into view. There they are: my mother and my grandmother, both dressed in silk dresses, sitting across from each other, sharing half a chocolate pecan pie. My mother is lounging with her feet up on the ottoman, but Grandmother, as always, sits up straight and proper, as if her spine were made of iron. I was right about the drink too: Although it's ten o'clock on Saturday morning, a big pitcher of mimosas is within easy reach of my mother.

"There you are! Aren't you precious? And isn't that a tasteful coat?"

"Thanks, Grandmother. You actually gave it to—"

"As if I don't remember, child. Anything to see the end of that foul thing you used to drape over your shoulders. Honestly, it is sometimes such a struggle with you."

"Such a struggle," my mother parrots.

"But we certainly were rewarded for our efforts at the Christmas Ball. You were the most gorgeous debutante ever!"

"Well, Madison looked pretty great too," I say.

"Pshaw! Blondes win over brunettes every time."

"And Alex—"

"Don't even speak that name in this house," my mother says.

"Dorothy Lee's prodigal granddaughter is a disaster waiting to happen," my grandmother adds. "She's as common as pig tracks. Just her being here lowers the tone of the entire city."

"That's hardly fair. She's my friend—"

"Not fair?" my mother gasps. "Have you completely forgotten what she did to Thaddeus? She put a love charm on him. He could have died."

"Madison did the same thing to Thaddeus, and you don't hate her."

"Because Madison does not have a malicious bone in her body," my grandmother says, revealing just how little she knows about Madison. I love Madison, but some of the things she says would strip paint. "Hers was simply the misguided act of a young girl blinded by a teenage crush. What Alex did was a deliberate attempt to destroy this family."

"I've spent a lot of time with her," I say. "She's not like that. She'd never hurt Thaddeus on purpose."

"Hayes," my mother says, "can't you see what she's doing? They can kick Magnolias out, you know. If you associate with a bad element, the League will cut you loose so fast you won't even have time to bleed."

"Oh, Ellie, don't be so dramatic." My grandmother sighs. "Now you're scaring her."

"Well, maybe it's high time someone started being dramatic," my mother says, pouring herself another mimosa. "Alex Lee is a disgrace, an embarrassment, and an obstacle to Hayes."

"Only if her grandmother continues as president of the League, and that's hardly a foregone conclusion. Now quit your jaw music. I know what's in my grandchild's best interests."

"They may be your grandchildren, but they're my children, and I'll do whatever it takes to protect them," my mother says.

"Do Jesus, Ellie, I heard you the first time." My grandmother sighs again. "Now hush up before you start wearing on my nerves. Hayes, if you're going out, make sure you're at 404 Habersham by one forty-five. I know you have a tendency to lollygag, and it will not do for you to be late for your first League meeting."

"But I'm never—"

"Don't back-talk me, miss. We need you focused today. All eyes will be watching you as the most promising young Magnolia we have, and I expect you not to disappoint me."

My cheeks go red. "I won't."

"Because your mother is not entirely wrong, you know. Even a broken clock is right twice a day. Magnolia League membership *isn't* a given. Not forever. You have to continue to earn your spot."

"I—"

"So you take that seriously, yes?"

"Of course."

"Good. Because without the League, you'd be nothing."

I swallow hard and nod.

"All right. One forty-five, Hayes."

She turns her back to me as she reaches for the pitcher, indicating that this conversation is over. Seizing the opportunity, I smile at her and my mother and slip out the door before they can start squabbling again.

My grandmother—who discovered Alex's ill-advised plan to put a Come With Me, Boy on my poor brother, Thad—has advised me to sever all ties with my new friend other than unavoidable Magnolia business. Sybil is a wise woman, correct on just about everything besides the color peach and Michael Bolton, and it's true that Alex has pulled some less-than-savory moves. She attempted to dose my brother with that love spell, she lied to Madison, she deceived me, and recently she's inexplicably started acting like some kind of super-perfect League member. I mean—what? She just got here.

But the bottom line is that Alex is a Magnolia sister. I believe in a lot of things—God, our country, the concept that *y'all* is the correct and most polite way to address a group of people — but above all, I believe in the League. My membership has given me everything I've ever wanted. I'm pretty, I'm popular at school, I basically have no problems, and I'm dating a gorgeous boy. If I were just *me*, well, who even knows what I'd be?

Winter in Savannah is truly amazing. The cold air takes the edge off the swampy breezes, and people can actually walk a few blocks without being drenched in perspiration. Everyone is always out in the parks no matter what the weather, but especially on a day like today. Several of the local ladies have taken the opportunity to celebrate the mid-fifties temperature by dressing their dogs in sweet little sweaters that match their own coats.

The only item on my morning agenda is a Christmas gift return. Jason gave me a book on golf. Golf! At first I thought it was strange but cute that he would give me a book on the sport *he* likes to play. Then I realized he was regifting me! Which is why I am nipping by to see the reasonable ladies at E. Shaver's to do a little exchange. *Madame Bovary, bien sûr.*

The rate at which my hoodoo love charm is wearing off Jason is alarming. I had to dose him for flirting with another girl, and the result was, well, annoying. He always wanted to kiss me, always wanted to be around. But now he's treating me in a totally second-rate manner, which will not do. As soon as this Magnolia meeting is over, I have to speak to Sam or Sina about another batch.

After purchasing my book, I make my way up through Madison Square to my favorite part of Savannah— Broughton Street, a lovely stretch a few blocks from the river just packed full of the cutest little shops and cafés, not to mention Leopold's Ice Cream. I start off my morning with a chocolate brownie sundae, complete with butterscotch, whipped cream, and candied pecans, then make my way to my favorite boutiques—Copper Penny for shoes, James Gunn for cocktail dresses. Then, before going into BleuBelle's to see what's new, I pause to catch my reflection in a store window. It's always good to keep an eye on things. My hair, which Sybil had me conjure as long and blonde, is radiant from the Ever-Shine, and the Calorie Canaries seem to have been working overtime, because I'm looking even trimmer than usual. As for my complexion, I've kept up the deer-tick paste regimen Sina prescribed and, I have to say, despite the concoction's disgusting texture, it's cleared every blemish from my face, as promised. I am a Buzzard-created beauty, head to toe.

"Hayes!"

I whirl around. It's Anna, in all-new Christmas clothes.

"Hey, Anna! How was your holiday, sweetie?"

"Great! My dad got me a Vespa. It's super cute. You should come for a ride."

"Does it have a matching helmet?"

"Helmet? Who wants helmet hair? Besides, I'm a good driver."

I've seen Anna drive, and she's like a squirrel on Adderall behind the wheel, but it's not my place to judge. Alex and Madison make fun of Anna enough, calling her Orang-Anna, a reference to her ill-advised self-tanning routine.

"Well, be careful."

"So, what's the gossip?"

I've always liked Anna, but according to my mother, her family is complete New Money, and my grandmother has pointed out on several occasions that they're not even really Southern. She claims Anna was born in Delaware or something. Still, Anna prides herself on knowing everything before anyone else does. She's not all bad.

"Oh, Anna, you know I don't gossip!"

"And you call yourself a Southerner. Well, the whole school is talking about your friend Alex."

What? "Why?"

"First she comes to town looking like something that crawled out of one of those natural, organic food barns. Then she gets it together and lands your super-hot brother. Then she dumps him—I mean, your brother! And we're all sitting around thinking that she totally blew her social life, doing that, but it's like…

she's, like, doing this phoenix-rising-from-the-ashes thing, you know? I mean, she's everywhere around town over vacation—every ball, every wedding, every charity event—right at her grandmother's side. Everyone's just waiting to see who she lands next, and what she'll do. Did you see that thing on her in 'Savannah Seen'? It's, like, she's only sixteen, you know, and she's the biggest thing the Magnolia League has ever turned out."

"That's a bit of an exaggeration."

"Not as far as I can tell. And you don't have any inside dirt on why she gave Thad the boot?"

I bristle. I may have my issues with Alex, but we're both in the League, and that means something. It means Alex and Madison will always have my back and I will always have theirs. If I can't trust that, then what is the League but a bunch of gossipy old ladies?

"No, Anna. Because, really, it's none of my business."

"The heartache of your brother and your best friend? I mean, Hayes, if it's not *your* business, then whose business is it?"

She has a point. But still...

"Anna, I just can't say any more. Magnolia loyalty. You understand."

Anna nods. "I get it. Although what I don't get, Hayesie, is why you bother keeping up with that League stuff. It made sense when you were obviously going to be the head of it. But what if Alex changes it all around? I mean, her grandmother has been running it forever, and obviously Alex is going to be in charge next. Where does that leave you?"

My heart hammers inside my chest as I think of my grandmother's words this morning: *Without the League, you're nothing.*

"I guess you have Jason."

"Oh yes," I answer, grimly thinking of his half-hearted presentation of *Swing Now!* wrapped in newspaper at our Christmas tea. "Anna, it's so sweet of you to be concerned for me, but I've got to go. Important Magnolia meeting this afternoon. I'll see you in school, okay?"

"Okay," she says, with what I can't help seeing as a crafty smile as she saunters off. It's all I can do to run into BleuBelle's and have Damien show me the latest clothes that fall within the River School dress code. Shopping always helps, of course. After a few outfits I'm barely thinking about Anna anymore.

But really . . . what if she's right?

2

Alex

On the first Saturday of the new year, my grandmother and I sit across from each other at the Gryphon
Tea Room, on the grandest section of Bull Street.
We've been engrossed in polite conversation for more
than an hour now, although, because of our carefully
hushed tones, the other diners can't hear a word of
what we're saying. Still, everyone in the restaurant has
noticed us, not least of all the few tourists who've wandered in for brunch.

You can tell my grandmother is used to being stared at; she almost seems to invite it. After all, who sits in the main window of the Gryphon Tea Room if they don't want to be noticed? That's probably why we're dressed so well. The other diners most likely wonder how we can fit into these threads, having just ordered a *second* tea platter stacked with little frosted vanilla cakes, warm, buttery scones, and tiny pimento-cheese sandwiches with the crusts sliced off—a feast that might challenge a party of four.

Of course, what very few Savannah natives would know is that just four months ago, I looked a lot more like a Bob Marley wannabe, complete with awesome dreads, than this picture-perfect debutante princess. Four months ago, I probably would have been politely asked to leave the Gryph because they'd think I was there to sell pot in the bathroom.

But people can change. Or that's what I'm trying to convince my grandmother of. So here I am, hanging on her every word.

"You must remember," she says to me, "that your appearance matters at all times. As a Magnolia, you are always onstage. Right now you've got a very nice look, but you spent *time* getting ready for the meeting today. The key is consistency. Consistency is what separates the merely well dressed from the impeccably turned out. One late-night run to Kroger in your sweatpants for some small emergency item, and your image is ruined. All that hard work goes up the chimney because of a weak moment."

I can't help smiling. "I'm sorry, but that's *crazy*."

"Might be. Doesn't make it any less true, though. I once wore a bathrobe to pick up the newspaper, and Khaki caught a glimpse of me on her morning walk. She gave me hell about it for weeks. I got so sick of listening to her that I finally had Doc whip up a Saw Nothing powder that I slipped into her biscuit. Believe me, Alexandria, people remember your looking bad *much* longer than they remember your looking good. And you, my dear, have a long and unfortunate history of disagreeable clothing and fashion choices to live down."

I shift uncomfortably.

"It's why plastic surgery after the fact is almost always a bad idea. People remember. The key is prevention. And prevention is precisely what League members strive for."

"Miss Lee?" My grandmother has forbidden me to call her Grandmother. "Sometimes I think you are the wisest person I know."

"Don't play me for a fool," my grandmother says. "It's insulting that you think I wouldn't notice your sass."

"I'm sorry. I just meant that all this is new to me. I get lost sometimes."

I give her my most honest expression. My grandmother looks at me cautiously, narrowing her eyes as if testing my sincerity. But I've become good at this—without flinching, I hold her gaze. Finally, she sits back and takes a satisfied sip of tea.

"Hmm," she says.

Ha!

Alex: 1. Evil grandmother: 0.

Okay. You may be wondering why a former Birks-wearing, Phish-loving, California hippie like me is now

    a. dressing like a Bush twin,

    b. being a fake, syrupy poseur,

    c. ditching my homey Dex, who happens to be waiting at the library now, and

    d. bothering to listen to something as dumb as debutante protocol.

The fact is I'm in a serious jam. It's pretty freakin' bad, though it does, maybe, have a silver lining. The good news is that my mother, who for a whole year I thought was dead and gone, is actually alive. Well, sort of alive. Half alive? Whatever she is, she's not dead yet. Her van *did* go over the edge of Orr Springs Road back in Ukiah, and her body—well, it *did* technically stop living. But her spirit hasn't actually gone over to fully dead yet, which means, in a way, she might be able to come back to me again. I know that sounds crazy, but I've seen her.

The bad news is that my grandmother has bought a hoodoo spell in order to keep my mom's spirit prisoner. Spells calling on the dead are strictly forbidden to the Magnolias, so I don't know what she thought she was doing or how she was able to do it. She doesn't have a clue that I know, so my entire perfect Southern princess act is just to win her trust until I can find a way to set my mother free.

"Alexandria," Miss Lee says, "pay attention! *Where is your mind, child?*"

Um . . . Hades? Soul-raising tactics? "Oh, I was just thinking about how gorgeous your floral arrangements are this week."

She looks at me suspiciously. "Have you been dabbling with Sina again?"

"No! I—"

"Because you know that any association with her or Sam Buzzard outside the League is strictly forbidden."

"Oh yes. I know," I say innocently, desperately hoping she hasn't been checking my phone records. Sina is my only hope to lift the spell off my mother. I've been talking to Sina more than anyone.

"Fine. Now. Your clothes of late have been quite appropriate, even I must admit. Other than that silver . . . thing. You cannot wear that."

I can't help frowning. "But Madison designed that cocktail dress herself. I think it looks cool."

"It really doesn't matter what you think," Miss Lee

snaps. "You are in training, and therefore your personal taste and opinions are not to be trusted until they are fully and reliably shaped—by me. Perhaps the other girls can get away with these trashy Music Television looks, but they're not born to leadership. You need to look appropriate."

I finger the hem of my dress. In fact, Miss Lee has done away with *most* of the awesome wardrobe Madison and Hayes picked out for me back in the fall. They gave me a makeover so extensive I'm kind of surprised *Teen Vogue* didn't fly in to document it. I thought that would be enough for my grandmother, but ever since I told her off at the Christmas Ball, I've had to undergo a whole other transformation. Now I'm so damn preppy, I look like a walking Episcopal church social.

But this is her game, and I'm playing to win.

"All right." I give her a bright smile. "I really appreciate your guidance, Miss Lee." I smile again, then sneak a glance at my thin antique watch—a gift from Mary Oglethorpe.

My grandmother catches me. "Going somewhere?" she asks.

"I just…" I hesitate. I consider a lie, but the truth is so harmless I decide to let it fly. "I was actually going to meet Dexter from school at the library real quick. It's the first time he's read *The Lord of the Rings*, and I—"

"Absolutely not."

"But—"

"Fantasy games are unbecoming to a lady," she says, closing the subject. "And the idea that you would even dream of spending time with some strange boy when you could be reinforcing your relationship with your Magnolia compatriots leaves me breathless. You are going to have to earn the respect of the other girls."

"Hayes and Mad *do* respect me," I say, trying to recover. "We're sisters. Don't you remember how they had my back when I walked the stairs at the ball?"

Which, it becomes instantly apparent, is exactly the wrong thing to say.

"I remember very well, Alexandria," Miss Lee says coldly. "I remember those humiliating antics of yours perfectly."

I clench my hands in my lap. Crap, crap, *crap*.

My grandmother's eyes bore into me in a way that makes me seriously uncomfortable. Then, just as suddenly, her face transforms into a terrifyingly false smile.

"Why, is that *Jonathan Bailey*?" She raps sharply on the window, and a large man outside, trailed by a miniature version of himself, grins and heads inside the Gryph.

Quadruple crap. My grandmother may be concerned about propriety in every other aspect of her life, but with Jonathan Bailey that goes clear out the window. She's working on some lucrative business deal with him and persists in throwing me at his son, Owen, an oafish, paw-heavy redneck known by all the girls at school as SlOwen.

"Well, I was wondering when you two would show up," Miss Lee coos. "Alex here has been dying to see Owen." My heart sinks. Apparently, my grandmother has set me up—again.

SlOwen grins at me. He reeks of Axe body spray, and I try not to wrinkle my nose too obviously. It's one of the first things a Magnolia League debutante learns: Keep your thoughts and opinions to yourself. No matter what you may think about someone, keep it on the inside. On the last date we had (at Miss Lee's insistence), he dragged me out to St. Catherines Island at five a.m. to go whitetail hunting. We sat in the deer blind for five hours in total silence. I'm an animal rights advocate and, at least in my old life, a PETA member, so if a deer had come anywhere near Owen's gun, I was prepared to throw a shoe at it. But the only animal we saw all day was a squirrel, and that was while Owen was passed out from his third midmorning beer, anyway. The dude still managed to wake up enough to try to paw me on the way home. Just thinking about it makes my skin crawl.

Keep it on the inside, I remind myself.

"Hey," Owen says, pointedly looking at my chest. "You look really ... flowery."

"Owen dear, Alex was just telling me what a *wonderful* time she had with you last week. You just charmed the pants off her with that hunting trip!"

"Hope you're being literal about that!" bellows his dad. "Ha! Girl's got legs that go on all day, including Sunday!"

"Oh, Johnny. You *are* hilarious. Well, Alexandria, Johnny and I have some business to discuss, and I know you've been dying to catch up with Owen. Why don't you two keep each other company while we old relics talk about boring, grown-up money things."

"But Miss Lee, my plans..."

"What plans? I'm sure Owen can show you a better time than that Dexter person of yours. You two run along."

Owen wipes his nose with his sleeve, then drapes a thick tentacle over my shoulder. "Some kids are over at Wet Willie's right now," he informs me. "They've got girls who're supposed to wrestle in Jell-O —"

"Excellent, Oren. No need for details!"

"Owen."

"Now, Johnny, shall we?"

Nodding at his dad, Owen ushers me out the door, his arm clamped around me. Just to play the part, I wink at my grandmother and then turn to Owen to give him a *you-are-so-awesome* smile. Which, of course, is exactly when Thaddeus Anderson comes striding around the corner of Charlton Street, his skin tan against a white button-down, blond hair sliding in front of his green eyes.

Oh God. Just looking at him makes my heart want to explode. Seriously. I'm afraid it might actually burst. He looks pleasantly surprised to see me, which makes me feel like I'm floating up like a big balloon. It's just like it was before, when he came down from his superhot-guy platform to tell super-normal and awkward girl Alex that he thought she was cool. The way he used to look at me — as if I were spinning a plate on one finger and running naked, covered in paint, down Bull Street. As if I were the funniest, weirdest girl in the world — that's how he used to look at me. I used to be able to make him laugh just by making a stupid face. But he's not laughing now. Instead, a horrible, cold mask slides down over his face, and I remember what I did and how much he hates me. I don't blame him. If I were him, I'd hate me too.

"Oh," he says, stopping. "Hi." His eyes travel from me to Owen and back to me. The neutral expression he's trying to maintain is clearly a struggle. "I —"

"Hey, man," Owen says. "Lookin' forward to seeing you play sticks this spring. Wanna come to Wet Willie's? The daiquiris are off the hook, and Alex and I" — his hand slips down my back and he squeezes my side protectively, fingers creeping closer and closer to my breast—"are heading over to get our Saturday morning drink on."

"No," Thaddeus says quickly. "I'm cutting down, myself. See you in school." And with that he turns on his heel and strides away from us.

I feel sick. Really. I think I might throw up.

"Buzzkill!" Owen calls at Thad's retreating back. He turns to me, grinning. "Right? I mean, dude. What a *snob*."

It takes a major effort, but I manage a tiny smile. "Right," I say, desperate to banish my ex-boyfriend's pained face from my mind. I watch him walk away, blinking back the tears before Owen can see them.

Every nerve in my body says to run after Thaddeus and tell him everything. But I know there's no way he can know the truth.

3

Hayes

Magnolia League Meeting, Number 437
Miss Lee presiding
Refreshments: Mrs. Funche (savories), Mrs. Basinger
(sweets), Miss Oglethorpe (beverages)

I've been at 404 Habersham plenty of times, but only
once during a meeting of the Magnolia League and
never as a member. Ever since I was old enough to

write a thank-you note, I've been told that this building is here waiting for me. It's been my Buckingham Palace, my White House, my Taj Mahal, so coming here today as a real member is — well, it's a big deal. Alex and Madison may feel differently, but for me it's one of the greatest days of my life.

Outside it's winter; but inside the meeting room, it looks like spring has exploded. All the members of the Magnolia League are packed in tight, wearing every pastel shade under the sun. Enormous arrangements of hydrangeas sit on the side tables and mantelpieces like giant pink and purple fireworks. And just about every flat surface is buried beneath piles of pickled shrimp, cheese straws, deviled eggs, and smoked-ham biscuits. There's scuppernong punch, coffee, mimosas, Bloody Marys, cherry bounce, and two pitchers of some mystery drink that tastes absolutely delicious.

Today, at last, we're the main event — Madison, Alex, and I. The first new members in three years, we also happen to be the grandchildren of the Senior Four. Now that we're finally here, everyone wants to welcome us, say a few words, kiss our cheeks, give us hugs.

Tinkle tinkle tinkle. Tinkle tinkle tinkle.

With one perfectly manicured hand, Dorothy Lee, Alex's grandmother, is ringing a tiny china service bell. Conversation instantly screeches to a halt.

"Thank you all so much for joining us today for

the four hundred and thirty-seventh meeting of the Magnolia League of Savannah," Dorothy says. "I apologize that there aren't enough chairs, but it's so rare that we're all together at the same time. I expect we can tolerate a little discomfort. Besides, after the holidays, all this standing is good exercise."

"Standing isn't actually an exercise," Madison whispers, and I give her an unladylike elbow in the ribs.

"Before we move on to new business, we *must* do our root list. I have the following members listed as due to have their roots and charms renewed this month: Julie Buchanan, Sadie Funche, Hayes Anderson, Marjorie Basinger, and Albertha Legree. Please, all of you, remember that you need to provide Sam with *all* of the required ingredients for your youth renewals."

"That is going to be extremely difficult," my mother says. "Some of those items are impossible to source right now."

"Goofer dirt is very low," Mary Oglethorpe, the treasurer, says. "Particularly for the financial-sector charms."

"I thought old Sean O'Reilly passed last week. The vice president of Georgia Commonwealth Bank? Didn't anyone go to his funeral?" Dorothy asks.

"I did," my mother admits. "But what should I have done? Gather the dirt in my purse? I think people would have wondered what I was doing."

"In other words, you were off to the wake too fast," my grandmother quips.

"Well, someone has to go to the grave tonight," Dorothy says. "How about one of our new girls?"

"I'll do it," Alex volunteers. Madison and I exchange glances. It really is a little annoying how much of a Magnolia Alex is trying to be lately.

"That's wonderful, Alexandria," Miss Lee says, looking pleased. "Now...did anyone who is scheduled for a renewal not hear her name read out? No?"

Sandy, Madison's mother, raises her hand.

"I'd like a *new* youth renewal," Sandy says. "I've been getting a little frayed around the edges. I think my charms might be...unraveling."

Miss Lee frowns. "Are you sticking with the regimen?"

"Well, I'm a working woman and—"

"The noontime prayers are *not* optional, dear. If you go to Sam, that's the first thing he'll tell you."

"But I've been mostly doing them—"

"Mostly isn't always. We can't waste the Buzzards' time with silly requests. I'm sorry, but no. Anyone else?"

I look over at Mrs. Telfair. Her face has turned a deep shade of crimson.

"Well..." It's Mary Oglethorpe. "I was going to ask for a bit more Prosperity Oil. Not Sam's. Sina's. Sina's is noticeably more potent."

Miss Lee turns to Mary and gives her a cold stare. "Mary, you *must* learn to control your spending."

"I—"

"Ladies, we are all given the appropriate proportion of Prosperity Oil every year. We are extremely fortunate—extremely!—to have this oil in today's economy. But you have to exercise more judgment in using it. You cannot throw it about promiscuously, as if it were drinking water. I'm afraid I'm going to have to say no, Mary. But perhaps one of your sisters will lend you what you need?"

"I have a little bit set by," my grandmother says. "Tom's practice has done extremely well this year."

"Thank you, Sybil." Mary sniffs, giving Miss Lee a look that could kill a mule.

"Anyone else?" Miss Lee asks sweetly. No one dares to speak. "Excellent. Well done. I'm glad to see so many of you are managing your charms so well. Now, I have an irregular item I'd like to bring before the membership today. Does anyone object?"

It's evident from the expression on my grandmother's face that her vote would be to throw Dorothy Lee and her irregular item right into the river, but no one objects.

"As all of you know, I lost my daughter a little less than a year ago," Dorothy says. Little sympathetic sighs bloom quietly around the room. Next to me, I feel Alex stiffen. "Well, I've been working with Jonathan Bailey to arrange an appropriate memorial gesture. Louisa loved gardening and horticulture, as most of you probably recall. Representatives of the Park and Tree Department of Savannah have told me that the current greenhouse is not meeting their needs, and so I've purchased the vacant lot at the end of Habersham Street. That's where they'll build the Louisa Lee Memorial Greenhouse. My daughter would have...she would have liked a greener Savannah. And...and she..."

Dorothy trails off. In sixteen years, I've never seen her forget what she intended to say next. No one even dares to breathe.

"The first anniversary of my daughter's passing is less than two months from now," Dorothy manages. "It will not be a happy day for me. I would like something to distract me from it. I've never used the League to pursue my own agenda, but I'd like to have a small reception here that night, just as a quiet fund-raiser. Vote?"

"Seconded," Khaki Pettit says.

"All in favor?" Mary Oglethorpe asks.

"Aye," say thirty-four voices in unison.

"Thank you all so much," Dorothy Lee replies, with what seems like real emotion.

A buzz spreads through the room. There's nothing like seeing a grown woman come close to tears to create a minor sensation.

"Order," my grandmother suddenly calls. "The room will come to order, please." I can't help wincing at the sound of that "please." It's like the crack of a whip. "This is a wonderful way to start the year, but let us please all keep our dignity. What Dorothy has requested is simply not appropriate."

The room falls silent. Mary, Khaki, and Dorothy look at her, stunned.

"An event at 404 Habersham reflects on the entire League, past and present," my grandmother continues. "When has the Magnolia League ever held a little bitty reception for anyone? We might as well just put out a folding table, eat off paper napkins, and call ourselves the Rotarians. No, if we're going to raise funds for the Louisa Lee Memorial Greenhouse, then let's do it in style! We probably won't be able to have a ball on such short notice, but at the very least it should be a soiree."

It seems that Dorothy is about to say something, but suddenly Sadie Funche chimes in. "Seconded!" she cries.

"All in favor?" asks my grandmother.

The "ayes" blow the roof off. Voices are ringing out all over the room, and committee assignments are being made, and I just can't help myself: Before anyone can stop me, I've volunteered Alex, Madison, and myself to handle the flowers, ticket sales, and music.

Finally, the meeting adjourns early, and the room sighs with relief. All the Magnolias are buzzing, and the only thing anyone wants to talk about is the fundraiser. Who's planning what? How are we handling food? Can we do this by February? Even though it's the middle of the day, I decide I'll have a sip of something, and I'm just turning to get a mimosa when Madison rises up in front of me like an accusing ghost.

"Do you know what you just did?" she asks, proceeding to toss back a Bloody Mary. "Do we need to have an intervention? Because I have to assume you're on crack."

"Oh, come on, Mads. Don't hose on my parade."

"You just threw us under the bus," Madison says. "I'm not about to spend the next two months of my junior year as some decoration slave. And Alex doesn't look so thrilled about this either."

"We're doing this for Alex's mom. It's a wonderful cause."

"My mother is *not* a cause," Alex says, coming up behind us. Her eyes are full of tears. Before I can reply, she pushes her way out of the room.

"Nicely done," Madison says.

"Well..." I'm trying to recover, but I don't know what to say. Madison and I take a couple of ham biscuits and head downstairs after Alex. We find her outside, sitting on the steps.

"You know, you're going to have a big black mark on your butt when you get up," Madison says.

"I want to be alone right now."

"Look, you think we're happy about this soiree thing?" Madison asks. "We don't really want to volunteer. Hayes just let her mouth get away with her."

"It's my mother we're selling tickets for," Alex says.

"Like she's, I don't know, a carnival ride or something. She's barely even dead!"

"Time out," I say curtly. "Enough of this pity party. Your grandmother thinks showing emotion is unladylike. Didn't you see her up there? I've known your grandmother all my life, and that's the closest I've ever seen her come to crying. Besides, who knows? If you support her on this, you two might actually grow closer. Would that be such a terrible thing?"

Alex's face looks positively at war with itself. Her mouth wants to say something angry, while her forehead scrunches up, like she's thinking hard.

"You're right," she says, relenting. "I just...it's tough, you know?"

"I know," Madison says, putting an arm around Alex's shoulders. "That's why we brought you ham."

"*There* you all are." My grandmother is coming down the stairs. "I am so *delighted* that you girls took on such an important challenge. I know you'll make me proud."

"It's all Hayes, Mrs. McPhillips," Madison says.

"I don't believe that for a skinny minute. I know that both of you are just being the sweetest and most supportive dears to your friend in her time of need."

Sybil stops and cups Alex's cheeks a bit tightly with one of her gloved hands.

"You look just like your mother," she says, and then turns. "Hayes, why don't you ride with me?"

It's not a suggestion; it's an order. And so I follow her to the car, which is parked, as always, in the No Parking zone. No one would dream of giving my grandmother a parking ticket so close to 404 Habersham.

"*Damn it all to hell,*" my grandmother suddenly hisses before even backing out of the parking lot.

"Don't worry," I say quickly. "The flowers won't be a problem. I've—"

"Are you blind?" she snaps. "It's not the *flowers.* This is another of Dorothy Lee's power grabs. She thinks the League is her own personal *playpen.*"

"She just wants to do something nice—"

"Don't give me that. She's the reason Louisa left in the first place. I could just spit, seeing her up there, squeezing crocodile tears out of her dusty old eyes. What a show. And lording her grief over the rest of us, as if she's somehow more profound than anyone else, when she practically killed her own daughter."

I sit quietly. That notion seems pretty unreasonable to me. After all, it's not like Dorothy drove Louisa over that cliff.

"Hayes, I want you to keep an eye on your chubby little friend."

"Alex?"

"Do you have other formerly fat friends I'm not aware of? Of course, Alex. Alexandria Lee. What a horrible name. It sounds like she's from West Virginia.

You and I, we're going to make sure this is the last time Dorothy Lee treats the Magnolia League like she's the queen of the Nile. This party is going to be the end of her, and you're going to help me."

Suddenly, Dorothy Lee's face appears at my grandmother's window. I can't help jumping.

"I was just talking about you," my grandmother says, beaming as she lowers her window. "And how brave you were to speak about your private grief in such a public forum."

Dorothy's not having any of it.

"I saw you sneak that handkerchief of mine, Sybil. Give it back. We all know perfectly well what you like to do with other people's things."

I look at my grandmother questioningly. Handkerchiefs and other personal items can be used to cast curses on someone. Was Grandmother planning to make some kind of Miss Lee hoodoo doll?

"Oh, how silly! I forgot all about it." My grandmother laughs, reaches into her purse, and pulls out the offending hanky. "I'm turning into you, Dorothy. Taking things that don't belong to me."

"Like my daughter's memorial," Dorothy says, snatching it from her hand. "Who would think of turning a simple service into a ball? This is Savannah, Sybil, not Las Vegas."

"Sister," my grandmother replies with a smile, "I am no more capable of making those women do a dern thing than I am of teaching a cat to dance. All I did was call for a vote."

"The last time I checked, the Magnolia League was *not* a democracy. Thank God."

"Maybe it should be," my grandmother says. "Then you could take a rest from having to run it all the time. How many years has it been? They're starting to show."

I'm trying my best to disappear. I don't even know where to look.

"Hayes," Dorothy says.

"Yes, ma'am?" It comes out as a squeak.

"Your grandmother has always had a streak of ugly on her. Take care you don't let it wash off on you."

Then she turns and walks away. I venture a look at my grandmother. She's breathing hard through her nose, staring straight ahead. Then she's out the door and flying up the street. I go after her. She catches up with Dorothy just as Miss Lee is getting into her car. Alex is sitting in the passenger seat, looking right at me. I am mortified.

"How *dare* you act holier than thou," my grandmother snaps. "Sitting on your throne, snapping your fingers, and watching everyone jump. Parsing out your spells like a miser at a banquet. As if everyone didn't already go around you when they really needed something. As if your own precious granddaughter didn't go running off to Sina so she could put a love spell on my grandson."

Dorothy laughs. "You think I don't know about Sina's side business? I'm *thrilled* about it. If I had to hear every little want from you ninnies all the time, I'd be dead from exhaustion. It doesn't trouble me in the slightest that y'all cover yourselves in nickel charms and dime elixirs like they were cheap perfume. And if you think I don't keep track of all of them, you're sillier than I thought. I know everything you do, and the second a Magnolia asks for one of The Three, I'll be on you so fast you'll feel like you just got hit by a downtown bus."

The Three. When the Magnolia League was founded, Doc Buzzard told the Magnolias that they could not, under any circumstances, cast one of The Three: the Sister, the Future, or the Dead. No spell or root may be taken against a Magnolia sister; no Magnolia may ask to see the future; and no Magnolia may attempt to raise, trap, or communicate with the dead. I don't know what happens if you do, but it's definitely not good.

"You'll what? Go to Doc Buzzard and put a Blue Root on us all? Oh, but you already did that, didn't you? And who ended up dying? Your own *daughter*."

My grandmother must have had one Bloody Mary too many. I just can't let her go on in this "less than" way. I hate to intervene, but it's the right thing to do.

"Grandmother," I say sweetly, "we're going to be

late for that appointment back at the house. With the upholsterer?"

Sybil whirls around.

"Don't even talk to me, you manufactured little idiot," she snaps. Alex's mouth drops open. Even Dorothy flinches at the venom in my grandmother's voice. "Volunteering, indeed. You think I'm actually going to let you near any of the details of this fund-raiser without supervision? You're just not bright enough, sugar. You take too much after your mother, and that's the truth. Now hush up and march yourself back to the car. This is grown-up talk."

I can't speak. My entire face feels numb. Not bright enough? I make all A's! She's always criticized me in person, but never in front of other people before. All I can think to do is wave politely and run back to the car before she can say anything else. As I retreat down the street, I can still hear them talking.

"Good God, Sybil. How did you ever get to be so hateful?" Dorothy asks. "You know, I still remember you when you were just a sweet little fifteen-year-old ugly duckling in a hand-me-down sundress."

And then my grandmother says the strangest thing.

"How did I get to be so hateful?" Sybil spits. "Why, sister Dorothy! *You* know how. You taught me everything I needed to learn about hate that night at Tybee Island. I learned it all from you."

4

Alex

After my grandmother and Sybil finish their street brawl, my grandmother drives us back home without saying a word. The air in the car is heavy with unanswered questions. Like, what the hell happened between those two to make them hate each other so much? That's not my main problem this afternoon, though. What's really bothering me is how my grandmother could want to turn my mom's death into a party. It's just all so ... *gross.*

All I want is my mom back. I'd trade everything in this stupid house just to have another hour with her. Give me our drafty, mildewy cabin at the commune. Take away my shiny, no-frizz hair and my Marc Jacobs clothes forever. Let me be heavy and awkward for the rest of my life. Just give me sixty more minutes with my mother. Honestly, I'd give up my whole life for that.

I catch sight of myself in the mirror. What would my mom say if she could see me right now, with my new, perfect body, symmetrical features, and super-model hair? Would she even recognize me? I look at my hand. The scar I had from when she accidentally cut me with her pruning shears is gone. My mom *gave* me that scar. I had it all my life. Would she even believe I'm her daughter without it? Suddenly, I just want the old, average Alex back so badly that I ache inside.

"What are you doing in the dark?" my grandmother says from the doorway as she switches on the light. "Admiring yourself?"

"I'm not doing anything."

"Mirrors are for self-maintenance only. Not for mooning over like a cat in love with herself. Now—"

"Excuse me, I'm really tired." I push past her. "I'm going to lie down."

I run upstairs and close my door and pull my blanket up over me. I know I blew another opportunity to make my grandmother trust me, but I just want to be asleep and not hear her voice and not think about any of this for a little while.

The next morning, I wake up totally back in the saddle. I manage to act perfectly at breakfast and the rest of the day, and somehow I keep my mask from slipping. I also force myself to stay away from Hayes. I wanted to call her as soon as I woke up, but Hayes is super private. She likes to maintain the illusion that everything is always peaches and cream, so I *know* she won't want to talk about what happened. She'll get in touch with me when she feels that enough time has passed so no one will mention her getting reamed in public like that.

That afternoon, I try to figure out what this half-century-old White Glove War could possibly be about.

"We just have our differences," Miss Lee says.

"What kind of differences?"

"Oh, who cares, Alexandria? It's a rift we can't mend."

"Never?"

"No."

"Well, she must have done something pretty terrible to—"

"Just take it as a lesson learned. Whatever you do, preserve your friendship with your Magnolia sisters.

Once you lose that alliance, you have to protect yourself even more."

"How can I protect myself if you won't tell me who I'm protecting myself from?" I ask, sitting in her lavish dressing room. She's getting ready to go to a Savannah Philharmonic concert with Jonathan Bailey. Her freshly lipsticked mouth takes a sharp downward turn.

"Well, haints, obviously. Slip-skins, plat-eyes. Roots. You know the basics by now, darling."

"But who would bother putting a root on me?"

"Well, that's the question, isn't it? Just be smart. Personal items expose you to danger. When you get your hair or nails done, you need to make sure to take the clippings with you. I can't remember the last time I licked a stamp, and the reason I have my handkerchiefs, gloves, and umbrellas monogrammed is not to help me remember my initials. It's to make sure that no one ever takes them."

"Or what?"

"Good Lord, child. Haven't you listened to anything I've said? When you have power, you have enemies. Women like Sybil are just waiting to get their hands on something of mine so they can put the bite on me."

"So I'm protecting myself from Sybil McPhillips?"

She looks at me carefully. "Listen, m'dear. About those accusations she made the other day. Anything

Sybil McPhillips said about your mother was said with one purpose, and one purpose only: to hurt me. There's not an ounce of truth in any of it."

"I know."

"I would never hurt your mother. Or you."

Except that you are hurting my mother.

"Okay."

"Try not to sound like an abused child, Alexandria. Sulking is unpleasant and will give you wrinkles. Now go."

My grandmother then shoos me out so that she can do whatever secret hoodoo herbology she needs to conjure her youthful-looking face into place. Josie is in the kitchen frying chicken, and the house smells delicious, but I'm not hungry. When Josie calls me for dinner, I just take a couple of pieces and go back to my room.

I sit on the floor next to the wall where my mom's spirit is trapped. Recently, she's been moving around a lot, and not just at night. As the anniversary of the day she had her car accident gets closer, her soul is more and more restless, as if she can sense it coming. I tap lightly on the wall three times with the tip of one finger, hoping my mom can hear me.

Boom!

I jump back, terrified, as something on the other side of the wall smashes into it.

My grandmother's heels race down the hall. I make it to my bed just in time.

"What was that sound?" my grandmother asks, standing in my doorway. She looks severe and imposing in her floor-length green gown and silver jewelry.

"Maybe something fell over in the other room?" I offer, trying to sound innocent. "You want me to go check?"

"No, thank you," my grandmother says. "And what have I told you about eating in your bed? It's reserved for the elderly and the infirm."

"I'm not feeling well," I lie.

"I don't have time for your moodiness. Good night, child."

"Good night, Miss Lee."

She nods and closes my door. I hear her shoes click down the stairs, and the front door shuts. Then I run to my window to watch until she's gotten into her waiting town car and disappeared down the block.

The moment I'm certain she's gone, I resort to my old tactic for getting into the Blue Room—breaking and entering. I head to the porch, flip my legs over the railing, and take that perilous step over the forty feet of free fall to the brick driveway. Then I set my foot on the drainpipe and hop onto the ledge of the porch next to the Blue Room window. Is the window still unlocked? Yes! Phew. I slide it up and dive inside.

"Mom?"

There's no question that something is there. I hear a light knocking on the ceiling. When I look up, I see a tiny cluster of what look like fireflies circling and buzzing above. They swirl and dance, growing brighter, then dimmer, finally uniting to become as bright as a close-up star. I have to shield my eyes from the light.

"Louisa Lee, are you here?"

It's nearly dark outside. I stand up and close the curtains. Almost immediately, I hear an audible sigh of relief, and then a strangled scream and the sound of something like a sack of coins hitting the floor.

"Mom?"

And then...she's here. She's *here*. My mom, the beautiful, gorgeous Louisa Lee. But she's as white as snow, and her skin looks damp. Her eyes are so dark I can't tell what color they are. She's so thin I can see her bones.

"Mom?"

"Who are you?" She backs away. "Get out!"

I flinch, but I know not to panic—she acted the same way last time. According to Sina, Mom's trapped in some kind of bubble that's not in the present, and she doesn't know where she is. I straighten up, trying to sound confident. "Louisa, listen to me."

Her eyes get bigger. She whimpers like a child.

"You're going to be okay."

"I want Sam," she says in a small, pitiful voice. "Where's Sam?"

Does she mean Sam Buzzard? Her childhood friend? "I can bring him."

"I want Alex."

My heart leaps. "I'm right here, Mom."

She shakes her head, beginning to sob. "Alex? Where is my Alex?"

I swallow, trying to stay calm. "I'll bring her, okay?"

My mother sits on the floor, putting her head on her knees.

"Mom?" I approach slowly. The last time I touched her, she threw me against a wall. I lay my hand on her shoulder. It's ice-cold and spongy. My stomach turns. How are we going to make her normal again?

She looks up at me. Her eyes are streaming yellow tears. "I want to go home," she whispers.

"Just hang on."

I look at my watch. Miss Lee's been gone twenty minutes. I need to get out of the room before Josie comes upstairs. If she catches me in here, she'll tell my grandmother, and it'll all be over. "I'll be back soon, okay?"

She puts her head down and sobs again. I squeeze her shoulder one more time. I guess it hurts, because she snaps her head up and snarls. I know she's my mom and would never hurt me, but it seriously scares the bejesus out of me. I ease out the window, swing over the drain-pipe to my porch, and slide back into my room.

All right. This is it. The only thing I care about is getting my mom out of here. That's all that matters. I need the house empty for at least a couple of hours to do it.

Wait. *Of course.*

The night of the greenhouse fund-raiser. The one time both my grandmother and Josie will definitely be out of the house for at least five hours. So what I need to do is *not* protest this sick party. Instead, I need to make sure it happens—majorly. All of Savannah will be there…so Sina and I can be here, setting my mom free.

It's time to get Madison and Hayes involved. I was keeping them out of it because I was afraid of a leak, but there's no way I can pull this off alone. And though a few months ago I'd never have believed it, they're the only two people alive whom I trust.

Magnolia sisters forever, until death do us part. Or beyond, apparently.

5

Hayes

This first week of school after winter break hasn't been so bad, but I'm still pretty shaken up. I know I disappoint my grandmother sometimes, and she's often had to speak sharply to me before, but the fact that she said those things in front of the Lees...It's been a week, but every morning the words echo inside my head, and I just feel myself shrinking until I'm this tiny, scurrying little bug, ready to be stepped on again and again.

I don't really feel like going to any of the parties this weekend, but Jason keeps getting more distant, and I need to be around to keep an eye on him. If I don't get a good gris-gris together and slip it to him, I'll be boyfriendless. The problem is that the ingredients are really hard to come by, and I've been so distracted by League politics that I've fallen behind.

But face time is important too. It's very unlike me to shoehorn myself into other people's plans, but when he tells me on Friday that he's going to Pinkie Master's Lounge, I can't help suggesting that I accompany him.

"Well, it's just a few of us going," he says. "Lacrosse guys mostly."

"Jason, I've hardly seen you all week. Pick me up at eight, okay?"

He doesn't. I call him twice, but there's no answer. Lord, what is wrong with me? Why did I have to wait so long to renew his love charm? Now putting a new spell on him is going to be more difficult than ever.

To distract myself, I decide to practice a little magic. I've simply got to get a clue as to what could possibly be causing my grandmother and Dorothy to spit such venom at each other. Reaching behind a row of my favorite books, I pull out an old shoe box with a tiny magnolia painted on the lid, and then extract a cotton bag of hazelnuts and acorns. I sit on the floor of my room and light three white spirit candles, each one wrapped with a single strand of my hair. Rolling the nuts in my fingers, I think of Hayes Mary McCord. According to the rules of The Three, I am absolutely not allowed to call on the dead. But every Magnolia has a soul spirit—a dearly departed one whom they draw upon. We're not allowed to conjure them, but we can channel their energy for answers. So though we've never actually spoken, I've been asking Big Hayes for guidance for years.

> *Big Hayes, Big Hayes, please guide me.*
> *I have a question, what do you see?*
> *My grandmother and Dorothy, so full of hate,*
> *Is the problem little, or is it great?*

I blow on the acorns four times, close my eyes, and drop them onto the floor. I can hear them rolling. After a moment, I open my eyes. The nuts have formed a large, scattered circle. Big, my soul spirit means. It's not a spat. The problem goes deep.

Taking a deep breath, I gather the acorns and put them in a jar to be purified with thyme. Then I put two white pieces of paper on the floor. On one I write *Dorothy*. On the other, *Sybil*. Then I take out the hazelnuts and roll them in my hand.

Big Hayes, Big Hayes, please guide me.
I have a question, what do you see?
This rift between the grandmothers of Alex and me,
Who is to blame? Who could it be?

Shutting my eyes, I drop the hazelnuts. But this time there is no neat formation. Instead, the nuts go crazy, rolling all over the place, scattering all the way to the walls and even making it to the door. I hear someone coming, and I scramble, gathering them up.

The door opens.

"Please knock!" I snap, not looking up.

"Pretend I did," says Thaddeus.

"What do you want?"

He looks disapprovingly at the candles and my kneeling position. Having been the victim of one—and almost two—love charms, Thaddeus is not a fan of magic.

"Dropped an earring," I say.

"Uh-huh." He sighs, then walks to my bookshelf, his hands behind his back. He pretends to read the titles, but since they're all in French, I know he's faking. "Hayes, are you trying to *become* Carla Bruni? Your French isn't good enough to read all these."

"I'm just preparing for when Dad comes home from France. He'll probably have a new wife."

"Right," Thaddeus says. He doesn't like to talk about Claude. "See Alex at the meeting the other day?"

"Of course. She *is* a Magnolia."

"She seem all right?"

"She seemed fine." I hate it when Thaddeus asks me about Alex. I don't want to encourage his pining, and I have no clue why she dumped him.

"I saw her with Owen Bailey the other day."

"What? Gross! Anyway, why should you care?"

"The point isn't why, Hayes. The point is that I *do*."

"I—"

Before I can unravel that fortune cookie, my phone rings. Thaddeus picks it up and looks at the screen. "Speak of the devil."

Oh God. Why does the timing always work this way? She's probably calling to ask how we're going to start organizing for the fund-raiser. Naturally, I'll be in charge.

"I've got to take this." I push him out of the room and close the door. He's probably listening on the other side, so I walk over to my bed before answering.

"Hey," Alex says. "So glad you picked up. Listen, about last week—"

"There's nothing to say about that," I answer quickly. "Just a misunderstanding. Grandmother wasn't feeling herself."

"Sure, she wasn't," Alex says. "Look...I wanted to know if you'd run an errand with me tomorrow? Madison has plans with Dex or something, but I have something really superimportant I need to talk to you about."

"An errand? Alex! You know I hate errands unless they involve shopping."

She laughs. "Well, I'm sorry. But your mother asked me to drive all the way out to Hardeeville to pick up some sweetgrass baskets for the silent auction. An errand for your grandmother or something. The least you can do is ride with."

"Really?" That's weird. When did Mom ask Alex to do that? And why didn't Sybil ask *me*?

"Will you come?"

"Oh, all right."

"Thanks, Hayes," Alex says. "Seriously, I appreciate it. You're saving my life."

The next day is another crisp, clear, fifty-five-degree winter day. I'm wearing the cutest scarf and sunglasses—very Grace Kelly. A few weeks ago, Dorothy gave Alex a little Mini Cooper convertible, and as cold as it is outdoors, Alex never puts the top up, so I need to be prepared.

I have to say, Alex's car *is* pretty great. It looks exactly like the one Audrey Hepburn drove in *Two for the Road*—except, well, it's completely different. But here's the thing: It's just not right for Alex. It doesn't suit her. At least, not the real her. When she arrived in our "postage stamp," she was constantly lecturing all of us about our lifestyles and going on about being "green" and only buying shoes made of hemp. She wore these terrible old T-shirts, and her hair looked like some kind of urchin perched on her head. She even got *me* to buy a Prius. Come to think of it, I'm still driving that tin can, while she gets to zip around in this sporty thing.

"Hi," I say, hopping in. She's pretending that she hasn't been mooning over my brother, but I know better. (Pining-for-man evidence: Emo soul ballads are playing in the car.) Well, she doesn't have to worry. I sent my brother on an errand so he wouldn't be anywhere near the house this afternoon.

"Hi," Alex says. She hesitates, then hugs me. "Oh, dude. I've missed hanging out! We've hardly talked since the Christmas Ball, except for that meeting, and that barely counts. I've been jonesing for a download."

Jonesing! You can take the girl out of California, but you can't take the California out of the girl.

"It's good to see you too."

I pull back from her golden-retriever-puppy embrace. And then, because I don't want her to take it the wrong way, I add, "But please don't say 'download' in place of 'talk' ever again." And then, begrudgingly, "All right. I've missed you too."

"What have you been doing?" she asks as she pulls out of the driveway.

"Oh, you know. Madison and Dexter are completely inseparable. It's cute but, between you and me, a teensy bit irritating. And I've now read everything Colette ever wrote. And I'm completely obsessed with Jazz Age Paris."

"Hazer, you are such a closet nerd. Now that you have the buzzard's rock, apply to Princeton or something. Or go to France!"

"Maybe. Though I can't bring myself to put that thing on, sweetie. It's so awful-looking. The chain is made of weeds. I'm more of a platinum type."

Alex's face suddenly gets serious. "Hayes, that is my dead mother's most prized possession. Not to mention the most powerful thing the Buzzards ever made."

"Relax. It's in a very safe place."

"So, have you thought about how to use it?"

"No. And I might not use it at all."

"But, Hayes, you can leave Savannah now. You're protected from all evil. Don't you think you should do something with it?"

Really, she is driving me crazy. "Alex! Good Lord, I happen to like it here, okay? Now, I *command* you to swing by Two Smart Cookies, over here on White Bluff. All of this unnecessary conflict is making me hungry."

The truth is, the buzzard's rock *is* in a safe place — behind my collection of French novels. No one would ever think to look there, other than Thaddeus, who has rummaged through all of my things, as I have through his. As for the rock's significance, well, I understand that it is very powerful and all that, but I'm just not sure it's the sort of power I particularly feel like using. After all, if I understand its power correctly, the rock makes the wearer immune to harm and the Buzzards' Curse. As in, I may leave Savannah without facing any consequences. However, no one is trying to harm me that I know of, and I don't *want* to leave. After all, everything I want is here.

Heading north on I-95, we munch on our kitten-shaped cookies in silence. It takes an even dozen — with a couple of brownies thrown in — to sustain us. The MGs are always starving, thanks to our Canaries. We can eat anything we want and never gain an ounce — just one of the many hoodoo tricks the Buzzards have devised to keep us young and pretty. Alex, I have to say, is looking great, if a little pale. Her shiny brown hair is blowing in the wind, and her drop pearl earrings are bobbing next to her cheeks.

"Look, I'm sorry," she finally says. "I don't want to bicker with you. The fact is, I really need your help."

"I can't get involved in the Thaddeus thing, Alex. I'm sorry, but after the Madison drama last year—"

"I'm not talking about Thaddeus," Alex says, her face grim. "It's over between us."

"Why?" I can't help asking, despite having proclaimed seconds ago that I wasn't going to get involved.

"You're the one who made the mistake, it seems to me. Why are you calling the shots?"

For a moment, she looks as if she might cry. "I can't explain," she says, shaking her head rather fiercely. "You wouldn't understand, and neither would he." She sighs. "But, Hayes, that's not what I need your help with."

"So what is it?"

She takes a deep breath. "You're going to think I'm crazy. But there's a reason I've been hanging out with my grandmother so much."

"All right." I flip the mirror down impatiently, smoothing color onto my lips. "Tell me."

Then, without warning, my lip gloss wand jams into my cheek. Shocked, I look at the road. Alex's eyes are narrowed. She's veered across the left-hand lane, and the car is now heading straight across the large, grassy median.

"Alex!" I scream. "What are you *doing*?"

She doesn't answer. Instead, a terrifying sneer spreads across her face.

The tires scream as they leave the grass and hit asphalt again. Horns are starting to go off all around us, and the big rig that's heading straight toward us lets out a blast on its air horn. In about three seconds, the truck is going to smash into Alex's car.

Now, I am not particularly known as a girl of action. More of the waited-on sort, really. However, the one thing we MGs can't buy from the Buzzards is immortality, and I don't especially feel like dying today. Reaching over Alex's body, I grab the steering wheel and yank it as hard as I can to the right. At the same time, I rip off my seat belt. The little car responds too quickly, causing me to crack my head against the window as the front wheels cut back onto the grassy median and the back end fishtails. Still, for the moment, I've saved us. The big rig screams past us, just inches from the Mini's front bumper.

Sliding over the gearshift and sort of sitting on Alex, I'm able to get one foot on the accelerator and the other on the brake. I press down firmly but smoothly. As soon as the car's tires find purchase, we begin racing toward traffic again, but at least now I'm in control. I ease on the brakes and turn gently away from the oncoming lanes. I make a long, slow turn and come to a stop in the grassy center of the highway, then slide out from between the wheel and Alex's writhing body.

"Alex!" I yell, just inches from her face.

Her eyes are open, but she looks...possessed.

"Alex?" I call. "Are you okay?"

She sits up slowly, rubbing her forehead.

"Hayes..." She looks at me, confused. "What happened?"

"Well, you were preparing to tell me all about some big secret or something. Then you led us on a suicide mission across the highway. Don't you remember?"

She shakes her head vehemently. "No! What?"

"You tried to kill me, you jerk!"

"I didn't... I wasn't..." Her face turns white. "I didn't mean to."

"Well, you did. What happened to you?"

Alex gives me a strange look. I could be wrong but, I have to say, she looks genuinely scared. I walk to the passenger side and get back in.

"Don't worry too much," I say, attempting to smooth my hair back into place. "You're just a lame driver. We're fine. Let's go get those baskets."

"Hayes, I want you to get the hell out of my car."

I look out at the road. It's a particularly bleak stretch of I-95.

"Very funny, Alex."

"I mean it. Get out."

I feel my head. Did I bump it harder than I thought? Am I imagining this?

"Alex, what are you talking about?"

"You..." Her eyes dart back and forth frantically. "It isn't safe."

"Well, it's much safer *in* the car than out of it."

She takes a deep breath. "I mean my *brain* isn't safe when I'm in your presence. Okay? I am just... sick of your selfish attitude."

"Excuse me?"

"All it is with you is *me, me, me*. You're so worried that I'm getting ahead in the League. Well, face it! I'm the heir, Barbie, not you! So step off!"

"Barbie?"

"You heard me." For all of her harsh words, she looks unsure of herself. "You need to get your own garden to hoe, okay? Get out."

"No way! Drive me home!"

Alex takes another deep breath. Is she turning pale? "You know what else? You are completely...fake. Your looks? Fake. The way your boyfriend worships you? All because of a spell. It's just sad, Hayes."

Sad! *Me?*

"So you want me out?"

"That's what I said, faker."

"Well, you've got it!"

I slam my way out of the car and then pause to take the last shot. "I wouldn't want to spend one more moment in this cheesy car, anyway."

"Thank God," Alex mumbles, looking genuinely relieved. Before she can drive off, I grab the door.

"I don't know who you think you are, or why you've suddenly turned into an ungrateful brat, but I will never forget this, Alex. I am a generous person. And I thought we were friends. But unless you apologize and drive me home, our friendship is over."

She just stares at me.

"So? Are you driving me home?"

"No," she says. "You're easy. You can find a ride."

I take a deep breath. "You know what this is going to mean for you? Socially? And at school?"

"Good," Alex says. Shocked, I back away from the door, and she peels away, leaving me alone on the litter-strewn highway to fend for myself.

6

Hayes

Attention, everyone: For the first time in my life, I have a real enemy. Her name? Alexandria Lee.

There I was, standing by the side of the road like a fool, watching Alex drive away. I've never gotten up close and personal with a highway before, and it's way more disgusting than I had previously assumed. There are dead squirrels, for starters, but that's to be expected. What appalled me the most were the huge drifts of cigarette butts, paper cups, hair balls, and beer cans scattered in the weeds.

Fortunately, Madison answered her phone when I called her to rescue me. Twenty minutes later, she drove up with a vial of Ladies' Fainting tincture, Sam Buzzard's special herbal supplement that is usually reserved for ladies who find out their husbands have been unfaithful. It smells disgusting but feels like a cool breeze going down. As soon as I was calmer, we immediately started discussing theories. Most of them revolved around Alex being hateful or on drugs.

"But it *could* be a crazy thing," Madison said thoughtfully. "You know, all this stuff with the anniversary of her mom's death."

"I don't buy it. Anyway, crazy doesn't have to mean rude. Or cruel. It was cruel to leave me there!"

"Totally," Madison said. "You might actually have had to walk somewhere. With your feet."

It was sort of sweet of her to make a joke of it. But all lightness flies out the window as soon as we get to Pulaski Square, where my mother and Sybil are holding court, planning the refreshments for the Louisa Lee Memorial Greenhouse Gala.

"She what?" my mother cries, her voice wavering. "She threw you out of her car?"

"Yes, but first she almost plowed us into traffic."

"My baby!" Mom wails, running for the Chardonnay.

"Why were you *in* Alexandria Lee's car?" my grandmother asks icily.

"Alex and I were running an errand. Your errand, actually..."

"*My* errand!" Sybil squawks with laughter. "Is that what she said? What a story! And then what happened, exactly?"

"She almost wrecked her car. I don't know...it was like she was possessed or something. She was just completely and totally out of it."

"Well, she always has seemed thin between the ears to me. Dumb girls are always bad drivers."

"Who's a dumb girl?" Thaddeus asks, sauntering in.

"Your former paramour," Madison replies.

"No, it wasn't like she was a bad driver," I say, trying to explain. "It's like something was making her deliberately steer toward oncoming traffic. And then afterward she was so...mean to me."

"Just say it," Madison says. "Mrs. McPhillips, she was a bitch."

"My baby!" my mom wails again.

"So, is she okay?" Thaddeus asks.

"Why don't you go ask her," Madison says impatiently. "Then ask her why she booted your sister out on I-95."

Thaddeus frowns. Once my mother starts crying into her drink, he slips out.

"Ellie, hush," Sybil commands. "As usual, you are being less than useful. Girls, I am not surprised by this turn of events. Not at all. Hayes, dear, listen to me now and cut her out of your life."

"I plan to. Out of everything but Magnolia business."

"Even that," my grandmother says. "You want nothing to do with her, do you hear? It's too dangerous for you to be near her."

Dangerous? Strange, that's what Alex said too.

And I thought that was the end of the discussion. But then Sybil comes by the next morning for coffee to tell me *again* to stay away from Alex.

"I cannot emphasize this enough," my grandmother says. "She is going to hurt you."

"Believe me, Grandmother," I say, spritzing myself with a little red pepper, bee pollen, and alligator blood to lift my spirits and strengthen my resolve, "I have *no* interest in forgiving Alex."

"This is not about forgiveness, Hayes. This is about *defeating* her. Do you understand?"

"Defeating...?"

"I want you to cut her *out*. Do you hear me? If she wants something, then you give her the opposite. If she says cold, you say hot. If she says black, you say white. Especially as it relates to this memorial event. Do what you can to see that she fails."

"All right," I say, picturing Alex driving her car away, leaving me stranded. "It's not really my style, but I'll do my best."

"Your *very* best, Hayes," she says, staring at me.

"I will, Grandmother. I promise."

7

Alex

I think it's finally happening. I think I'm actually going crazy.

I was ready to tell Hayes everything. I really was. I need her help. But then it was like something took over my body. My mind was on fire. All I could picture was blood. It was as if...I needed to *see* it or something. And I had the most overwhelming desire to kill Hayes.

I don't think it was me. It couldn't be. I would

never think that way. I think some evil soul was renting space in my body, breathing my air. The real me was...paralyzed.

Crap, crap, crap.

I'm still trying to piece together what happened. I was driving, we were talking, and then I saw a gray figure in the road. I swerved, thinking it was someone hitchhiking, and that's when...well.

Obviously, this vision was meant just for me, because Hayes didn't flinch. She wasn't even slightly aware that I was being enveloped by this putrid cloud. Oh yeah—it smelled like roadkill. I'm surprised I didn't throw up. And once it had pushed me aside and climbed into my body, it took me over. I was still in there, but I couldn't talk. You know that dream where you're trying to scream but nothing comes out? It was happening. Then suddenly it was gone, and Hayes was shaking me. And that's when I realized I had to get her as far away as possible. Because something is rooting me, and if she stuck around, I might kill us both.

Oh, Hayes. Why did you have to be so loyal? Those things I had to say...But if I hadn't gone for the jugular, she would have come trotting after me, trying to find out what was wrong. Because the truth is, she's one of the nicest people I know.

So now I'm rooted and my mom is still a prisoner. I've studied everything I could get my hands on—from weird underground pamphlets ordered on the Internet to dense, practically unreadable academic texts. I've waded through everything out there on voodoo, hoodoo, Yoruban magic, spirits, and death. Still, I have no idea how my grandmother could have trapped my mom's spirit. And I have even less idea about how to get her out.

"Alexaaaaaandria! Are you here?"

Oh God! I flop down on the canopied bed and pretend to read *Savannah Magazine*.

"Alexaaaaandria..."

"Up here!" I call out, listening as she climbs the stairs. In seconds, Miss Lee's thin, elegant frame is at my door.

"My Lord, *what* a mess! Everyone in town is talking about what happened between you and Hayes Anderson today."

"I told you, it was just a little misunderstanding—"

"Don't play me the fool," Dorothy snaps. "You threw Hayes Anderson out of your car. On the highway, no less! Sybil is ready to spit. I don't know what she did, but that's no way to act. Magnolia feuds never end well."

"What makes you think this is a feud?"

"This is *not* my first barbecue, child. You need to fix it."

I press my lips together. I will *not* put the MGs in danger. "I don't think I can."

Miss Lee narrows her eyes. "Here's what I know, Alexandria. Magnolias are a lot more powerful together than apart. We've had Magnolias stray—going out on their own, trying their own tricks. It always ends badly. Always."

"Like what's happening between you and Sybil now?"

Miss Lee looks at her rings. "What's between Sybil and me is not ideal, certainly. We have a long history and, unfortunately, the only things she ever wants are the things I already have. But that's no reason you and Hayes should repeat our mistakes."

"I'll do what I have to do to make this all better," I say. Pretty smart. It's the truth, but it means nothing.

"Changing topics—I was *very* pleased with how you stepped forward to take charge of the flowers for the greenhouse party."

"No problem," I say innocently, smoothing my skirt. "As long as it helped you out. I want to make this party big enough so everyone in town goes." I pause for a beat. "Although I am disappointed we haven't had more time to talk about, you know, Magnolia specifics and whatnot."

Miss Lee raises one eyebrow. "As in?"

"I dunno—*magic*. Isn't it time I started learning more about how this all works?"

"All in good time," my grandmother says.

I don't have time.

"But, Miss Lee—"

"Dinner is at six thirty. Please wear something

tasteful but informal. We've got company. And, Alexandria, when I say informal, you do understand that I don't mean smart casual or leisure attire, don't you?"

"Of course, Miss Lee."

I grit my teeth as I wait for my grandmother's footsteps to fade all the way down the hall. Crap. So now everyone knows about me and Hayes. Could things be any worse? Suddenly, there's a tap at the window—a pebble hitting it. After looking at my door to make certain it's closed, I run over to the window to take a look. When I see who's standing in the driveway, I have to steady myself at the windowsill.

"Thaddeus?" I whisper.

He waves. I open the window so fast I tear a fingernail.

"Hi," he calls from the ground, hands in his pockets. "I was going to ring the doorbell, but I didn't feel like making a grand entrance. Can you come down?"

Can I!

"Give me a minute."

I duck back inside. Oh my God. I've got cookie crumbs and Hayes's lip gloss all over me. I'd give anything to put on my old cutoffs and a tie-dyed tank right now, old-school Alex style. But if my grandmother saw me in that, my cover would be totally blown. I settle for a Billy Reid button-down Miss Lee bought me and khaki shorts. Perfect. I look like a Christian camp counselor. I'm downstairs in ten seconds flat.

"Hi," I say, hurrying toward the back of the garden, where he's leaning against the gate. His shoulders look wider than before, somehow. As usual, his ice-blue Sea Island cotton shirt is completely free of wrinkles, and his slightly worn Levi's fit perfectly. (Despite the designer jean trend, Thaddeus never deviates from the classics.) Either I'm fantasizing or he's actually growing hotter by the day.

We look at each other, then look away. There's so much to say, it feels best just to start with nothing.

"Let's walk," I finally manage.

We head toward the river, eventually wandering into Colonial Park Cemetery. As I walk beside him, I try not to wallow in memories of the beginning, when we first fell for each other. But it's impossible. I'm still completely in love with him. I steal a look. His shirt is slightly worn around the collar, and his eyes are so green they look like bottle glass. I have to pinch myself to resist the urge to throw my arms around him. No way, Alex. You almost killed Hayes just by being in the car with her. God knows what could happen to him.

"So...what's up?" I try my best to be icy, but instead I end up sounding like a frog.

"I just wanted to make sure you were okay. Hayes said that accident was pretty intense."

"There wasn't an accident. It was just a sticky steering wheel."

"Still..."

"I'm fine."

"I won't ask why you did that to my sister. I learned a long time ago that I can't ever figure Magnolias out. But it seems pretty low, leaving her alone on the highway like that."

My face turns red. "Yeah, well...you wouldn't understand."

"So that's how it's going to be?"

"That's how it has to be." I toe the ground with my sandal. "How are you doing, anyway?"

"Okay," he says curtly. Then, after a moment, "It's tough to see you right now."

"Sorry," I mumble. Oh, man. All I want to do is kiss him.

"As long as you're all right." He pauses on the sidewalk, looking at me. "Are you?"

I can't help it—my eyes fill with tears. Crap. I just want to tell him—someone—*everything*. "I..."

"Alex." His voice is urgent. And then his hand is on my wrist. It's amazing how just five fingers curling around my arm can set off a million little electric sparks all over my body. He leans in slightly, looking into my eyes. He's so close, I can smell the fabric softener his housekeeper used this week. My head begins to spin; a pleasant whir rises in my ears.

"Come on," he whispers. "You can talk to me."

"Oh God, Thaddeus, I—"

Suddenly, I hear a familiar, greedy hiss. Fear slices through me, instantly grounding me in our reality: *immediate danger.*

I turn to my right and there it is, hovering under a tree just a few feet away. The smell quickly follows. The gray shape buzzes like flies over a dead dog, and it makes hungry sucking sounds. I back away and chance a look at Thaddeus, who obviously can't see it.

It's coming for me. How do I know? *Because all I can do right now is picture Thaddeus dead.*

My heart is hammering in my chest. The monster drags itself across the ground more quickly than I thought it could move. It's rising up, almost as big as a person, and it's becoming more and more solid. I need to get away from Thaddeus, *now.* Once it's completely taken me over, I might do anything.

"I know what you're doing, Thaddeus." My voice is shaking. "This 'I'm concerned' act. It's very nice, but it won't work, okay? We're not getting back together. It's over. I have to go."

Thaddeus cocks his head. "I didn't say I *wanted* to get back together, Alex. Why would I possibly want to do that?"

"I—" The gray mist is coming into focus, looking more and more human.

"I don't even think you're a nice person anymore. This new look…the new *you*…it's really disappointing."

Despite the current seriously freaky and dangerous

circumstances, it's pretty hard to hear him say those words.

"Well then, we understand each other."

"Not quite," Thaddeus says. His face is starting to flush. "I came over to make sure you're doing all right. It's not like I don't care about you as a person. We were close, remember?"

All I can do is nod.

"But I don't know who you are anymore. This Magnolia thing you've bought into has turned you into something ugly, and that's too bad because you were a really smart, cool girl. But don't think for a second that I want to get back together. Because you're not cool anymore. You're just another one of *them*."

"Thaddeus..." I trail off. The mist has resolved into something almost solid. It looks like a man who's been underground for a long time. A fat man with gray clothes, gray skin, gray fingernails, gray hair. But not gray eyes. I can't see his eyes, because his eyelids are stitched shut. He opens his mouth and smiles. His teeth are black, and the tongue he runs over them is black and glistening too.

I want to hide behind Thaddeus and ask him if he sees this monster. But of course, I know he doesn't.

"Look," I almost shout, "I'm with Owen Bailey now, Thad. In fact, I've got to meet him right this minute."

He looks shocked and not a little pissed, but I can't

stick around. I sprint as fast as I can down the walkway and out of the cemetery. I think about the reading I've done. Okay, I don't know what the hell this thing is, but spirits hate three things: salt, corners, and puzzles. For now, corners and salt will have to do. I dodge from street to street, zigzagging my way toward the brackish river. The one time I look back, the creature is still there, closer than ever. Every one of his steps equals six of mine, and he's eating up the distance between us with his steady walk. I dodge around sightseeing carriages, through two squares, knocking over a flower vendor. Herds of tourists stop and stare; a couple of ladies in matching pink shirts stand up from a bench to snap pictures of me. I'd wave, but I'm running so fast now, my lungs are burning. Finally I make it to the river. Without bothering to take off my shoes, I take a running jump over the guardrail and splash into the freezing salty water.

I come up, gasping for breath. Several people have rushed to the railing to watch. I scan the shore. As far as I can tell, the creature is not one of them. He's gone. The cold January wind already has set my teeth chattering.

"You okay?" someone calls.

"Get the police!" another person yells. "She'll be hypothermic in minutes!"

The commotion grows louder as I swim toward the shore, hyperventilating from the cold. As I climb out, I see a reporter with a big camera. Oh, crap. I can see the headline now: *SPLASH! Magnolia Debutante Alexandria Lee, out for a January polar bear plunge.*

This will be a tough one to explain to my grandmother. But for the moment, I'm safe—and so is Thaddeus. And hard as it is to admit, in my heart that's what matters to me most of all.

8

Alex

I thought school was bad before, but now that Hayes and Madison have shut me out...well, I might as well be a ghost.

I show up late and I leave early. I don't talk to anyone before or between classes, and if people speak to me, I say just enough to get them to leave me alone.

Dex tried to take pity on me. He's Madison's love puppy now, but he was my friend first, and he never forgets it.

"Dude, you've been totally MIA," he says. "Plus, the Baby Maggots are all over your butt, man. And not in a good way. It's like you pepper-sprayed their Hanky Pankys or something."

"How do you know Madison wears—?"

"Never mind that, Junior. Tell the man what's up."

"Nothing," I say, eyes downcast.

"Come on. One session at Awful Waffle will cure you."

I wish, more than anything, that a triple order of smothered and chunked hash browns could, in fact, be the answer. But what if I go with him, for laughs, and then that monster following me somehow makes me stab my friend with a fork?

"Can't, Dex. Next time."

"All right," he says, obviously disappointed. "I actually wanted to talk to you about some stuff."

"I just really can't spend time doing that right now."

"Fine." He tosses his messenger bag over his shoulder. "I'm new at this dating scene and could use some advice. But whatever. I guess it's all about you, Slick."

I watch him walk off, my chest thumping. Will protecting my friends from this ghost-demon-curse-*whatever* cost me every single friend I have?

After that, I establish a pattern of isolation. I sit by myself behind the auditorium at lunch, daring the spirit to show itself. At night, I turn off my lights and stand in the middle of my bedroom waiting for it to appear. When I'm cutting through an alley, I turn around to see if I can catch it behind me. I never do. The closest I came was during lunch one day, when I felt my skin turn cold and hot at the same time, and I looked up to see the gray figure standing in the woods behind the science building, just staring at me. After a second or two, it melted back into the shadows and was gone.

On top of it all, jumping into the river on a freezing-cold day has done me far more damage than I imagined. Not because people think I'm crazy or something, but because they suddenly think I'm desperate for attention. When I crawled out, dripping wet, you could see my black bra right through my white shirt, and I think it gave everyone the wrong idea. At least, that's what I'm guessing, since I found a photocopy of the newspaper photo with *Bra goes on the inside, slut* or *Go back to California, tramp* or something similar written on it in marker and taped to my locker.

Anna was nice enough to fill me in one day when just the two of us were in the girls' room.

"It's just that you made such a giant display of yourself," she said. "And you flashed your chest all over the Life section of the paper."

"I didn't do it on purpose."

"Someone pushed you in?"

"Well, no, I jumped, but—"

"And now you've got lots of attention, exactly the way you wanted."

Then she flounced out.

As for Hayes, well, she's Hayes; she couldn't be rude in public if her life depended on it. But she is so icily polite to me, so aggressively proper, that it feels like getting freezing-cold water poured down my back every time I talk to her—

"Alexandria Lee!"

I look up, and Constance Taylor is standing right in front of my desk. A few of the boys laugh.

"If you don't find class interesting, then you may leave," she says. "You can spend the rest of the period in the front office or jumping in the river, whichever you prefer."

"But I wasn't doing anything—"

"Not true. You were daydreaming. Which is something, but in terms of AP English, no, you were not doing anything. You don't get a free pass for the rest of the year just because you have good grades. And that goes for all of you. Any one of you who thinks this is a class you can blow off, think again."

I force myself to pay attention until the bell rings. I've got to do better at staying below the radar, because if people notice me, they'll start asking questions, and then everything might come out.

"Alex, a word," Constance says from behind her desk after class.

I stand in front of her.

"Yes, ma'am?"

"Yes, *ma'am*?" she says. "Two months ago I couldn't get you to stop calling me Constance, and now you're suddenly so proper."

"I'm sorry," I mumble, trying to keep my head down. "Constance."

She rolls her eyes, then gets up and shuts the door.

"Alex," she says. "I know where you're from, and I know what you must be wrestling with. I'm sad about your mom too. And I did my best to out the Magnolia League, as you know. They are an elitist bunch of evil-doers. Literally. I thought we agreed on this. So, what's going on here?"

"They do good stuff. Community service, volunteer work."

"Your mother's memorial greenhouse."

I shrug, trying not to show how distasteful I think it is. "Sure."

"If something's going on, you can tell me," Constance says. "If you're in trouble, I want to help you."

"Why would I be in trouble?"

"Well, let's see. You stay in town after vowing to run away on the night of the Christmas Ball. You're joined at the hip with your grandmother, whom you hated not five weeks ago. You're suddenly a model member of the Magnolia League. You're avoiding your friends. You're doing ridiculous things in public, such as jumping into the river when, I have to assume, you were intoxicated. We've been back in school for only two weeks, but if you keep turning in work at the level you're currently doing, you can look forward to a B-minus at best for the trimester, and this is your favorite class."

I keep my head down.

"Alex, talk to me."

I want to. But what would happen? She's already lost one leg because of Magnolia League bad magic. And if she blows my cover about freeing my mom, all is lost.

"I really can't, Miss Taylor."

"All right, Alex. You win."

I turn from her desk.

"You know who you remind me of? Your grand-mother. And look how she turned out."

"Powerful?"

"Alone."

I try not to look too stung as I head out the door. But then—oh, great. Madison is waiting in the hall, tapping her foot.

"Alex, your presence is requested at the bench."

"I'm eating on my own today. I don't feel well."

"And I don't feel good about asking you, after the stunts you've been pulling, Judas. But Hayes says we need to talk about the ticket stuff and the party. The one for *your* mom. So you need to come."

"I've got homework."

"Liar," Madison says, putting her hand on my shoulder. "Now, march."

Short of physically assaulting her, I don't have a choice. Madison's strong; even though the Magnolias don't need to worry what they look like, I think she does some kind of boxing yoga for fun. She keeps one hand on my arm as she leads me out into the bright winter sunshine. It's a warm day, and people are eating outside—one of the nicer side effects of global warming. The only other person at the MG bench is Hayes, who pretends to read a notebook until I sit down.

"Alex!" she says, looking up. "I'm really glad you could make it. It's been almost two weeks, and we're *way* behind on this garden party thing."

"She didn't have a choice," Madison says, sitting next to me.

"So," Hayes says, "I know we're having our differences, but we need to talk seriously. There are just about twenty-eight days until this party, and I have no idea who's sold what in terms of tickets. And you have been MIA."

"I'm kind of preoccupied. It's hard to find time to just hang out."

"Alex," Hayes says, "you don't find time; you make time. Now, Madison and I have sold thirteen tickets between us, which is great, but that's not even close to half if we're talking one hundred people. We need to talk to all the Magnolia members and make sure each of them buys two. That's going to be a big source of sales. Right now, only a few have bought them. It's our first priority."

"I already did. I called them."

"You did?" Hayes is staring at me. "You called them? But we're the ticket committee. There is no *I* in committee."

"Actually, there is," Madison says.

"Alex, did everyone say no? Because if we can't get the Magnolias to buy the bulk of these tickets, it's going to be terrible."

"No, most bought them."

"How many?"

"Like, fifty."

"You've sold fifty tickets already? And they've paid?"

"Yes."

"Well, you can't just stuff the money under your mattress," Hayes says, thrilled that I've done something wrong. "You have to hand it over. That's not the way we use Magnolia funds."

"I already did it. I deposited the checks and cash and stuff."

Hayes looks like someone just told her that she was actually a giraffe. But it's true. Come hell or high water, I'm going to get everyone in town to this ball. That night, it's going to be all eyes on the party—no eyes on me. There's no way my grandmother will be able to leave before two in the morning.

"What else are you doing?" Hayes asks, her face completely white.

"I didn't mean to upset you—"

When Hayes gets upset, her entire face goes blank. "Madison," she says, "would you give us a minute?"

"What? I'm not old enough? Is this an adults-only conversation?"

"Madison?"

"Fine. I'd rather hang with Dexter anyway."

She strolls off backward, texting at the same time. It's quiet for a minute. A breeze kicks up in the trees. I cringe, sensing a showdown.

"Alex," Hayes says, her voice under supreme control. "What do you think you're doing?"

"I'm helping with my mom's memorial fund-raiser."

"I've only known you for a little while," Hayes goes on, "but this isn't you. You haven't been yourself since the Christmas Ball. What is going on?"

And then, to my surprise, she reaches across the table and puts her hand on mine.

"I don't want us to fight," she says. "I don't want to believe you're trying to hurt me. So tell me. What is it?"

And that's when I decide to tell Hayes. Not once in the entire time I've been in Savannah has Hayes not known what to do. Never has she been lost or confused, or hesitated for a second. She's been there for me. She's like the sister I never had. She's *good*. I really believe that she is. I haven't told anyone what's happening because I want to protect them, but I can tell Hayes. She doesn't need me to protect her. I need her to protect *me*.

So I tell her everything: about Sina, and about my blood pledge to help her break up the League in exchange for freeing my mother's soul. About how my grandmother has my mom's soul trapped. How someone has put a root on me, and that's why I almost wrecked the car. About the Gray Man and jumping in the river to get him away from Thad. How I'm trying so hard to be who my grandmother wants me to be because I can't have her suspicious of me while I try to free my mom. I tell Hayes how I don't want to make her and Madison feel bad. How I really want their help.

Or that's what I *want* to say. But when I open my mouth, it's like a stone is stuck in my throat. I try to talk, and I make a horrible gagging sound. Hayes pulls her hand back.

"Wait a minute," I manage to say. "I didn't mean that."

I try again. It sounds like I'm coughing up a hair ball. My throat is full of cold rocks, and I can't get words to come out around them. Hayes looks confused.

"Is this some kind of joke?" she asks.

"No. I'm—"

And then my throat closes tight again, and I can barely breathe.

"Should I get someone?" she asks. "Are you having another seizure?"

Then the words come out—thank God. But someone else is talking. They're not my words. "Why don't you go ask Sybil what to do? Since you clearly can't think for yourself."

I feel sick. He's back, and he's replacing my mouth with his own. My skin feels hot and cold all at once, the way it did in the car. I can't stop talking, even though I know the consequences will damage Hayes forever.

"Go kiss up the way you always do." I clap my hands over my mouth, but it doesn't help. "Everyone makes fun of you behind your back. No one in the League takes you seriously. You're just their mascot. They all think Madison is more talented than you, and I'm smarter. You're just a pretty face. Everyone feels sorry for you."

I'm shaking my head, trying to tell her it's not me saying these things. She just stares at me, her face red, and then one tear oozes down her cheek.

"I'm sorry. I'm sorry, but... *you're useless.*"

I get up and run. It's the only thing I can do to stop my mouth. I don't care who's watching.

When I'm halfway across the quad, someone grabs my arm.

"Alex?" Thaddeus asks. "What's wrong? What did you do?"

But I wrench myself out of his grip. I'm picturing him dead again, this time on the lawn. I don't want anyone near me now.

"Alex?" he calls. "Alex!"

I head to the one place he can't follow me: the girls' room. I slam the door behind me. No one else is inside. I lock myself into a cool, dark stall and pull my feet up so no one knows I'm in here. What have I done? I can't unsay those things I said to Hayes. I'm going to have to keep living as the person who said those terrible words to her. The person who made her cry. I lean against the stall and feel like crying myself, but all I'm capable of is one enormous, racking, dry sob.

Lunch will be over in twenty minutes, and I don't know how I'm going to face Thaddeus or Madison or Hayes. If I try to say anything to any of them, I know my throat is going to choke up all those horrible things again. And even worse, what if it wasn't a root? What if it's really how I feel? What if I said those things because deep down I think they're *true*?

The air splits open. A long, mechanical scream cuts through everything, drilling into my head, echoing in the bathroom. Then it changes to a series of whoops, then a long blast again.

Fire alarm.

"Anyone in the bathroom?" someone asks from the door. "Fire drill. Assemble on the quad."

I don't say anything, and the person goes away.

Outside the bathroom door I hear kids pushing and shuffling, and then eventually the sound fades. The alarm shuts off with a loud *click*, and then it's blessedly quiet.

The bathroom door opens. Someone walks inside. All around I can feel how empty the building is. I check to make sure no one can see my feet, and then I breathe quietly. Focused. Inhale quietly. Exhale quietly. I don't hear anyone walking around in the bathroom, and I wonder if the person left. But when I look down, a pair of men's feet is right outside the door of my stall.

His shoes are gray. The laces are gray. His pants are gray. I feel the bathroom filling up with cold air, and suddenly I can see my breath. And I can smell him again.

My heart contracts until it's a pinprick in my chest. I stop breathing. The feet just stay there. I stare at them, trying my best not to make any noise, but they don't move. Then the door of my stall rattles. Just a little at first, but then harder and harder. The sound is so loud someone must be able to hear it—but then I remember everyone is out on the quad for the fire drill.

It's a sudden, clear thought, and before it's even finished, I know what I have to do. I flip the latch and I fly out of the stall. The door hits something soft, something spongy, something that feels *dead*. But I don't look back. Book bag over one shoulder, feet slipping on the tiles, I burst out the bathroom door and run down the hall. The door to the outside is right in front of me. I'm almost there.

Then the door to the last classroom opens, and the creature steps out.

I try to stop, but I'm moving too fast, and I slip and fall. He senses me somehow, even though his eyes are sewn shut, and he begins to walk toward me, slowly, calmly, like we have all the time in the world.

I scramble to my feet and reverse direction. There's another door at the other end of the hall. I run for it. I don't know if he can teleport or if there is more than one of him or what, but there he is again, just waiting for me, already walking toward me from the other end.

I try the nearest classroom door, fling it open, and then trip over a desk and bruise my shins on the metal garbage can as I run for the windows. Sliding through the narrow window opening, I scrape my hip and thud onto the dirt and bushes on the other side.

When I look up, there's a pair of legs in front of me. But—okay! They're human.

I hear a familiar voice. "School can't be *that* bad."

"Sina! Oh, thank you, thank you, thank you. Get me out of here! There's a monster and—"

I turn around, but no one's there.

"He was right there. You've got to believe me."

"Oh, I believe you." Despite my distrust of Sina, I have to admit she looks breathtaking. Her brown skin shines against her tight yellow wrap sweater, and she appears queenly in her long skirt that reaches all the way to the ground. Her eyes are the color of newly mowed grass in spring, and her thick black hair is tied in intricate braids and wrapped in a fine silk scarf.

"You do?"

"And I know where he went," she says.

"Where?"

"He's hiding inside you right now," she says. "The Gray Man."

"Wh-who?"

"Come on. Let's get you to the Roost. It's the safest place for you while I sort this out. You need help, girl, and it's not the kind any of those Magnolias can give you. Whether you like it or not, you need me."

9

Hayes

My grandmother doesn't even knock. She just strolls right into my room and opens the curtains.

"I don't want the light on," I whisper.

"Why?" my grandmother asks. "Sitting in a dark room weeping over things that don't matter? You're better than that, my dear."

"I just want to be left alone."

I turn my back on my grandmother so I'm looking

out the window. She sits down on the edge of my bed and puts a hand on my arm.

"You're sixteen," she says. "It can't be all that bad."

In the blink of an eye I'm crying.

"Just let it out, sugar," my grandmother says softly. "There, there."

I'm not even sure what "there, there" means, but it makes me feel better when she says it like that. You know, my grandmother has a lot of faults, and she can be pushy sometimes...but I'm still her granddaughter, and she still loves me.

"Your mother told me you've been like this all week," she says. "Naturally, she thinks it's drugs."

Ha. Trust my mom to put down the Chardonnay long enough to call my grandmother and tell her I'm on drugs.

"I just had a fight with someone," I said. "And they said some mean things about me. Things that really hurt."

"Who?"

"No one. It was no big deal."

"It *is* a big deal, Hayes. No one makes my grand-daughter cry without me making it a big deal. Let me guess. It couldn't have been Madison—she doesn't have that meanness in her."

Right.

"I don't expect it was your brother, and your mother wouldn't have told me about it if it was her. So I'd have to say it was Alexandria Lee. There, how'd I do?"

I nod, and then I tell her the things Alex said about me. I can't help it; they just come pouring out. My grandmother doesn't interrupt. She just listens until I finish. Then she smiles and shakes her head.

"Those women take the skin off the people who are closest to them. Let me tell you something about the Lee family," she says. "There's a—how should I put this— a perversion that runs through them. A perversion of the *spirit*. Dorothy had it. And her mother had it. Alexandria's mother, Louisa, had it. And I hoped against hope when Alexandria came here that she might have been away long enough so the venom running through their veins had drained out of her. I saw you and Madison trying to be good influences, and I prayed that she was not like her mother or her grandmother. But, of course, I knew in my heart that the kitten grows up to be the cat."

"But why would she say things like that to me?" I really still don't understand it. It's like she was an entirely different person.

"Listen to me," my grandmother says. "Some things are out of your control. I want you to know that what came out of that girl's mouth was not about you. What's between Dorothy Lee and myself is not about you either. This started long before you were born."

"What's it all about, then?"

"I can't even go into it, m'dear. But I will tell you, it is the goal of the Lees to keep us in our place. Whatever Alex is doing, it's working. Do you feel small? Worthless?"

"Yes," I admit.

"And that's exactly the way she wants you to feel. Which is why you need to distance yourself from her altogether."

"Why are you still civil to Miss Lee, then? I mean, sort of."

"Haven't you ever heard the expression 'Keep your friends close and your enemies closer'? Well, that's my thinking."

"So she's your enemy?"

"I think the good Lord put me here so that one day when the time was right, I'd deliver Dorothy Lee her due comeuppance."

She hands me a starched handkerchief. I dab my face and sit up straight. I'm feeling a little better, I guess. More...resolved, or something. "And...do you think the time is right?"

"I let Dorothy Lee ruin my life," Sybil says. "But I'm not going to let her granddaughter ruin yours. Yes. I think the time is just about perfect."

She smiles at me — a glowing, almost otherworldly smile.

"So what do we do?" I ask, a little more eagerly than I'd like.

"Child, they can put Alexandria Lee in a ball gown, but it still doesn't change her upbringing. If we can't come up with something, then...well, then we don't deserve the Magnolia name."

10

Alex

Sina and I park in front of the hodgepodge of bunga-
lows that make up Buzzard's Roost. It's a beautiful
winter day in Georgia—the sky is wide and blue, and
the cool air is tinged with the delicious smell of wood-
smoke. A group of kids is playing ball in the courtyard
while two older women sit on a mattress swing, gos-
siping. The smell of Old Bay seasoning drifts through
the compound. Somewhere, not too far off, a guitar
lesson is going badly, competing with the radio music

flowing out a window. As soon as we walk toward the courtyard, we're surrounded by kids shouting questions:

"Sina, who's this?"

"Dorothy Lee's granddaughter."

"Moneybags!"

"How come she's here?"

"Mind your business. What's Greta got on for dinner?"

"Frogmore."

"Just keep moving," Sina says to me.

"Wanna play four square later?" one of the kids asks.

"If you'll teach me how," I say, smiling.

"I'll braid your hair."

"Don't you touch that hair!" Sina growls. "She paid me a lot to get it to look like that."

Giving the kids a sheepish wave, I trail after Sina to what I assume is Greta's house, a strangely designed bungalow that's part house, part maze, with multiple doors, a confusing little network of hallways, and a big, open room in the middle with a long wooden table, a fireplace, and floor-to-ceiling windows.

"Were all of these houses built at the same time?"

"No," says Sina. "You gotta earn a house at the Roost. Live here enough years, the family builds one for you. But the blueprints are all the same. Sam drew them up himself. See, these houses aren't just places to live; they're our protection against dead spirits and Blue Roots. 'Cept his house. His is one big, open room. But ours are designed special."

"What do you mean? It all just looks like a jumble someone made up as they went along."

"You see this fence around each house?" She points down at a tiny wall just a foot high. "Made of pure salt. Spirits hate salt. Reminds them of the tears they shed when they were still alive."

I bend down, touch one of the white slabs with my finger, and put it to my lips. It's tangy.

"But don't the fences just melt every time it rains?"

"Mostly, and then we come out and put up new ones. We paint our doors haint blue; that's a pretty obvious one. But you see how there's a conch over each door? Spirits hate the sound of the inside of a conch shell. All that roaring makes them run."

"What else?"

"Make the hallways zigzag. Spirits are easily confused—you know that. They like straight lines. That's why the walls have all those little doors that go nowhere. Lots of windows, lots of light. Clean all the time—dust is death. Literally. Gotta keep it out. And of course, we all keep a broom over the door."

Just then a large, older woman with a multicolored head scarf rumbles into the room, carrying a huge platter of food.

"Who's this?" Greta demands.

"Alex. My...client."

"Huh." Greta looks at me suspiciously. "One of those Magnolia children?"

"Naturally."

"Doc's not going to like it."

"Yeah, and when was the last time Doc even left his cave?"

"Humph." Her large chest rises and falls with disapproval. "You two better get yourselves served before those animals come to table. Won't be nothing left but claws and crumbs. Get yourself some Frogmore, Alex."

I can't help making a face. I don't mean to, but the idea of eating frog is just a little much.

"You got a problem with Frogmore stew?" Greta asks.

"Um..."

Sina laughs. "She thinks we're eating frogs. She thinks it's frogs for supper and possums for dessert."

"Nothing wrong with a nice, fat possum," Greta says. Then she glares at me. "Or a frog. All God's creatures taste like chicken. But there's none of them in Frogmore stew. Nothing in there except shrimp and sausage. Or you got a problem with shrimp and sausage too?"

"No. I mean, I used to be a vegetarian, but that's sort of impossible in my grandmother's house. And Georgia in general, it seems like."

"Oh, the animals know the order of things," Greta

says, heaping a mound of steaming rice onto my plate and topping it off with a thick pat of butter. Then she ladles chunky, steaming stew all around it. "You have to eat strong animals if you want to keep strong yourself. You think a thicket of collards gonna protect you from sickness?"

"I actually heard collard greens are pretty good for—"

"Ha. Thicken the blood with pork. Toughen the heart with beef. That's how I do it, and look at me."

"There's a lot to look at," Sina mutters.

"Hush up, you withered little catfish. Sneaky Sina, that's what we call her. What'd my sister do to get you here?"

"Your *sister*?" I look from one to the other. No outsider would ever believe that Greta was Sina's sister. Mother or aunt, maybe. But then I'd forgotten that Sina's conjured herself to look younger, just like the Magnolias. In reality, she's closer to Greta's age than to mine.

"We're just hanging out." Sina shoots me a look that says not to say a word about what's really going on. "She wants to know how to use her Come With Me, Boy with a little bit more subtlety."

"If I believe that, I'm Beyoncé. All right, little Sina. You keep on with your sneaky tricks. Just make sure she eats enough."

"Do you do magic too?" I can't help blurting out.

Greta laughs. "This little girl's been watching too many movies. She sounds like a tourist. Should I pose for a photo out back, little lady?"

"I'm sorry, I didn't mean anything."

"Don't be sorry. Just open your ears and maybe you'll learn something. We're regular people. Some of us know root work, and some of us know other kinds of things. Me? I can take a bag of flour, some tore-up old weeds, and half a pound of fatback and conjure up a supper for twelve. That's my magic. I don't need to fool around with my age or my luck or my love. I'm lucky enough, pretty enough, and young enough as it is. And I don't need a conjure bag to hold on to a man."

"Yeah, you just live off Daddy, that's all," Sina says.

"We live *near* Doc 'cause he's old and he needs us, you little crab. Eat your stew. You're such a skinny little shrimp that even a hungry shrimper would throw you back."

Suddenly, the room fills with noise as the children pour in and surround the table. Their shining voices bounce off the floor and walls.

"Frogmore!"

"Little Snake tried to steal my goofer spoon!"

"Did not!"

"Did!"

A wave of sadness washes over me. Until this moment, I'd forgotten what it's like to sit at a rowdy table full of people talking and jabbering at one another, bickering and arguing in a comforting, family way. It feels nice. Greta passes behind me and in one movement manages to refill my plate with more of that delicious, spicy stew. She grips my shoulder affectionately for a moment before moving on, like a giant cloud of short-tempered kindness.

"Well, we gotta be moving along," Sina says. "It's getting dark, and we got work to do."

"Magnolia's never going to get her lady curves by running away from a full table," Greta says.

"Leave it, Greta."

"You'll just conjure it off her anyway," Greta says. "Never saw the point."

Ignoring her sister, Sina leads me out of the house. It's quiet out in the Roost. Hearing the raucous supper in progress behind me only makes me feel like more of an outsider. I scuff acorns with my boots as I trudge across the sandy ground to Sina's house, and then I see an old friend coming out of the garden.

"Sam!" I cry, trotting over to him.

"What are you doing here?" he asks, disentangling himself from my hug. His soft shirt is dirty and grass-stained, as if he's been working in the garden. Faint smudges stand out under his amber-colored eyes; it seems he hasn't been sleeping well. Otherwise, he looks as handsome as usual.

"Sina was going to teach me some root work tonight. Basic love charms. And stuff. You know. Like that."

It's a bad lie, but Sam's too distracted to even bother calling me out on it.

"Here," he says, pulling me away from the garden.

"What's wrong?"

"Doc shouldn't hear you out here," he says. "Not this close to dark."

"Why?"

"Too many Magnolias around lately, asking for The Three."

"Calling the dead?"

"I think so. And I heard rumors that some are setting against sisters. You ladies seem to be having some internal troubles up in y'all's house."

"Who's doing it?" I ask.

"Can't tell you that," Sam says, a bit sadly. "Client confidentiality. But there's danger around."

Tell me about it. Apparently, it's already inside me.

"Alex!" Sina shouts from the doorway of her cottage. "Stop bothering Sam and come on!"

"See you soon," I say, giving him an apologetic smile and then shooting into Sina's house. Before entering, I pause at the threshold. I've been here before, but it always strikes me how weird the place is. There are doors of all sizes on the walls, and huge floor-to-ceiling windows. I bend down to try a small door barely as high as a toddler, but it won't open. Then I notice it's just a handle and hinges, cleverly worked into a painting of a door on the wall.

"Ha. You fell for it," she says. "All the dumbest ghosts do."

Despite the strange architecture, Sina's house is spare and elegant, everything swept clean, not a bit of dust anywhere, with carved wooden furniture. Tibetan rugs are scattered on the floor. Herbs hang drying from the ceiling, magazines and newspapers are scattered around, and old candles are melted onto most of the surfaces: windowsills, coffee table, the arms of the sofa, the exposed roof beams. Sina flips on some jazz and motions for me to sit.

"Tea?" she asks, putting the kettle on the stove.

"Nah. Thanks, though."

Sina turns off the burner, then pours herself a bourbon.

"All right," she says, sitting on the floor. "Let's get some things straight. I don't like the League. I don't like its history. And I really don't like that my family still lives out here while you parasites live in all those big houses downtown."

I look away, trying not to betray anything by my expression. But really—what *does* she like?

"I'm only helping you because we made a bargain, and that's how the world works: You accrue your debts and you pay them off. End of story."

"That's not true. There're other things, like love and friendship and—"

"Don't make me laugh," Sina says. "Love's just another way to pay for something nice you can't afford, and I'll take someone who honors their debts over someone who pretends to be my friend any day. We made a bargain, you and me; we owe each other something, and I always pay my bills. You can count on that more than you can count on any of your so-called friends. So that's where we are. We clear?"

"Crystal."

"All right, then," Sina says, "what kind of hoodoo you know?"

"Well, I know about herbs. I've done that Come With Me, Boy that I was supposed to use on Thaddeus. And I can make my own conjure bag."

"So you're a little tea-brewing monkey who's sat in on a few sessions and can parrot what the grown-ups do. About what I expected."

"*Hey.*" I know the smart thing to do would be to cool it right now, but I can't help myself. "I know a lot more than you think."

"I doubt that," Sina says, glaring at me over her glass. "You want to know hoodoo? The real thing? I can teach it to you if you want to learn. Because this'll sure go a whole lot easier if you actually know a few things, and by 'things' I mean useful things, not those jumped-up party tricks the Magnolia girls know."

I feel a prickle of excitement at the back of my neck. Ever since I've come to Savannah, people have been teaching me all kinds of things. How to dress and how to dance and which ball comes first in the year and who the head designer at Givenchy is and what fork to use and how to write a thank-you note. All things that I seriously couldn't care less about. Now, finally, someone wants to teach me something I actually want to *know.*

"You ready?"

"Yes!" I say. *"Yes."*

" 'Kay," she says, then polishes off her bourbon and wipes her mouth with the back of her hand. "First thing we need to do is get rid of whatever it is that's got its claws in you."

"How'd it even happen?"

"Someone conjured it."

"To follow me?"

She shakes her head. "To kill you."

I feel the words in my stomach, a dead, icy weight. As obvious as the notion is, I hadn't dared to let myself think it before. "Are you sure?"

"I'd say definitely."

I feel short of breath. "How? He wasn't going to, like, shoot me at school, was he?"

"There are all kinds of ways," Sina says. "But if it's the Gray Man that's got his teeth in you, he's the nastiest plat-eye there is."

"I never heard of plat-eyes killing anybody. I thought they were just spooks."

"Most are," she says. "But the Gray Man's worse than a spook. He's a nasty piece of business. Whoever conjured him on you really wants you gone."

"But how? A spirit's not real, right? It's just a physical projection of what my brain sees? At least that's what all the books that I've been reading say."

"And in the case of the Gray Man, that's pure destruction. He'll set you on everyone around you, and when he's done with them, he'll set you on yourself. Or maybe he'll be nice and start by letting you tear yourself up first."

"So in the car—"

"He was driving you to your death. Or maybe later he'd have you throwing yourself through a plate-glass window at school."

I can't say anything. An evil thought worms its way out of my brain and works its way down to my throat. "Do you think my mom's accident could have been the Gray Man?"

Sina's eyes widen briefly, and then she catches herself. It's clear she hasn't thought of that possibility— but it certainly could be true. "He doesn't normally travel that far. And we're not working on your mom right now. We're working on you."

"Okay." The whole thing makes my skin itch.

There's a dead man living inside me. It's like the world's most disgusting ringworm.

"All right." She rises and opens her huge wooden apothecary's cabinet. "No time for modesty. Need you to strip bare and put this on." She holds up a rough white cotton shift.

"Purification."

"You got it."

I duck behind a corner and put on the shift.

"Good." She hands me what looks like a moldy old penny. "Put this under your tongue."

"Sina, that looks disgusting."

"You want to get rid of the Gray Man or not?"

"Okay, okay." I brace myself and obey, instantly gagging. The coin tastes like a mildewed sneaker marinated in rotten cheese. It's so strong, it fills my entire head and trickles down my throat into my increasingly unsettled digestive tract. I feel like it's oozing out of my pores and stinking up the air around me.

"Now…" She moves quickly, taking candles, scraps of material, wine bottles, and various saucers off her long wooden table. "Lie down."

I climb up, then lie flat. Sina darts about with the fluidity and precision of a seasoned surgeon. She surrounds me with thick white candles, humming as she lights them with matches. It's growing dark outside by now, but the candles gently illuminate the room. Sina doesn't look me in the face. The nasty old coin is tasting worse and worse.

I feel a dangerous, unfamiliar rumbling in my stomach. Sina takes a jelly jar, fills it with bourbon, and places it next to my head. Instantly, the fumes make me dizzy. She places a plate of fresh bacon next to the jar. Compared with the horrible taste in my mouth, the bacon smells delicious. In spite of myself, I feel a pang of hunger.

I focus on the ceiling and try to think about anything else. The thought of the Gray Man worming his way up out of my stomach is more disgusting than I can bear. Sina takes out a big Ziploc freezer bag full of dollar bills, all of them caked with dirt and mud, and places the bag on my stomach. The rumbling is getting stronger now. My legs and belly are beginning to shake uncontrollably.

"Spirit!" Sina calls. "You in there, spirit?"

My hands are twitching, my shoulders bobbing up and down. The back of my head bangs against the table. Sina slides a folded dish towel under my skull so I won't give myself a concussion.

"Spirit!" she says in a loud voice. "Man up and show yourself! Who are you?"

And then I speak. But the voice that shoves its way out my mouth isn't mine.

"I need a drink, girl."

Sina smiles. "I'm no girl of yours. Do I look like your daughter? Who are you?"

"*Pirates need drinks!*"

"Name yourself and get a drink."

I can feel it — the *thing* pressing against the inside of my throat. It makes me feel like a cheap Halloween costume someone else happens to be wearing.

"*Take that penny out its mouth!*"

"No."

"*Take it out!*"

"We can do this all day," Sina says. "But you can't go forward, and you can't go back. You're just folded up, stuck inside that little bitty girl, and I know you want some whiskey. So just give me your name."

The thing inside me laughs ugly. My eyes seek out Sina's, trying to let her know that I'm still in here, too, that it's not me laughing, but she won't make eye contact.

"*You think you can trick me? I buried plenty of ones thought they were tricky like you. Buried them in secret graves.*"

"You sound so smart," Sina says, smiling. "Especially when you're cowering inside a dress-wearing girl."

"*Take this penny out my mouth. Watch me bite that smile off your face.*"

"I don't think you can," Sina says.

"*I took the smile off hundreds of faces prettier than yours. Cut 'em off. Ear to ear.*"

"Well, you're a big, bad ghost, ain't ya? But you ain't got no eyes."

"I got her eyes."

"Tell me this and I'll give you whiskey," she whispers. "Who rooted a big, strong man like you?"

"The lady," the voice gasps. *"Old lady. Looks young."*

"Well, that hardly narrows it down in this town," Sina says. She pours a bit of whiskey down my throat. I feel something wet run out of my mouth and trickle down my chin and neck. Something inside of me is squirming around, making me queasy.

"Come on, man. I'm getting bored," Sina says. "Let's get this party started. What's your name?"

"William . . . William Long."

"Okay," Sina says. "William Long. William Long, I'm calling you. Your sailors and your crew are looking for you. They're looking everywhere. I'm calling you up, William Long. Come on up out of this girl. Get some whiskey. Get some pork."

My body's shaking so hard I'm afraid I'll break something.

"Can't. Rooted."

The air in the cabin thickens, and suddenly the candles seem to give off less light. The shadows feel black and syrupy, as if the air itself is slowly turning into invisible mud.

"Caaaaan't."

It hurts so much. My body shakes harder. Sina

frowns. She begins pacing. The shaking subsides. She walks over to the kitchen cabinets, flings them open.

"Oh, Mr. Long. Look what I have here. I found you some brandy cake."

Suddenly, the shaking begins again, harder. I hold my breath and suck on the penny as hard as I can.

"Mmmmmm. Just a little taste." Sina turns and puts a big slice of cake in her mouth. Something rips itself out of my throat.

"*Ahhhhhhhhhhhhrrrrg!*" It's the worst sound in the world—a cross between a growl and a scream, and it's coming from *me*. It goes on and on and my throat feels raw and I don't think I can scream anymore. And then something breaks free inside of me. I feel smoke rise up out of my throat and the Gray Man emerges, a horrible cloud of death.

"*Caaaaaaaaaaaaaaaaake.*" He envelops the plate and Sina. Quick, and strong as a cobra, Sina throws the cake onto the floor. The wet, filth-encrusted spirit leaps and tears into it. Sina runs to me and covers me with a sheet painted haint blue.

"Lie still," she hisses at me. "You're dead."

I do what she says. The Gray Man continues to grunt and eat. Then there is a terrifying silence before he emits a sound of rage.

"*Give me back my little girl.*"

"She's gone, William Long."

"*Give me back my girl.*"

"Can't have her," Sina says. "Root's broken."

The Gray Man screams again. I cower under the stiff sheet. Then he stops.

"*Let me curl up inside you, then,*" he says, talking to Sina. "*Need your eyes.*"

"No, I don't believe I will," she says.

"*Come be one of Billy Long's girls,*" he says. I hear him take a step toward her.

"Off!" Sina shouts, and something heavy crashes into me. The entire table slides across the kitchen floor and hits the wall. Furniture shatters, and then I hear something breathing hard.

"*Hurts . . .*"

"Damn straight," Sina says. "I'm not one of your little girls, William Long. You don't want to fool with me. Now, get!"

"*Need some eyes,*" he whimpers.

"Plenty of eyes out there," Sina says. "But this one's not for you anymore, William Long. You go get some new eyes, then go home to your kin."

He screams and comes so near me I can smell cake mixed with the horrible stench of the grave. I clutch the sheet as tightly as I can.

"Take the whiskey, William Long. Take the money. Take the cake. And go."

There's a terrific crash as the Gray Man charges through the house, smashing glass and throwing things to the ground. I hear the sound of gulping, and then, with a final smash that must be one of Sina's huge windows, he's gone.

Neither of us moves for at least five minutes. It feels like an eternity. Then, finally, Sina takes off the sheet.

"He's gone," she says.

I shake my head, unable to say anything.

"Didn't say it would be fun. Last time I called out a spirit like that was in 1996. But you and me got a deal, and I take my bargains serious."

"So do I," I manage to croak. I feel worn out and hungover.

"I don't think any less of you 'cause you were scared," Sina says. "I was ready to start peeing in my britches myself."

I find myself smiling a little.

"Ugh. I *really* need a shower." Then it hits me. "Wait...where's he going?"

"He wants some fresh eyes. He'll take anything he can get now. Probably find a stray dog or a wild pig out there. Maybe a deer if he's lucky."

"What about the other Buzzards?"

"They all got charms on their houses," Sina says. "No Gray Man's getting in there."

"What if he comes across someone out on the road?" I ask.

"Well, that's just their bad luck, isn't it? Now go take a shower before you stink up my whole house."

"Sure." I rub my eyes. "I'm so tired, I could sleep a hundred years."

"Oh no, Miss Priss," Sina says. "No bed yet. We've got to plan your mama's second burial."

"We do?"

"We do."

"Won't it just be like the first one?"

"No. Second burial's different, and we have to do it before a year's been up or she's as good as stuck forever. The only way we can get her spirit out of the In Between is to hold a second burial attended by her kin."

It doesn't make much sense right now, but honestly I'm not sure that anything would make sense after having a ghost—or whatever the Gray Man is—ripped out of my body.

But something's still bothering me.

"So it sounds like it was a Magnolia who put the Gray Man on me, huh?" I ask.

"Sounds like it was your grandmama, that's how it sounds."

"You think she'd actually want me dead? I don't believe that for a second."

"You can believe what you want, but I'd advise you to start wearing that buzzard's rock twenty-four seven."

She leans over and picks up some broken glass. "Damn ghost," she mumbles. "I should charge you for the cleaning."

11

Hayes

In order to lift my mood out of the lowlands, Madison insists that I meet her at Anna's party. This is to be "the Mother of All Oyster Roasts," whatever that means, so this will be our weekend outing. Frankly, after Alex's cut-down, I would have preferred a nice quiet dinner out in the tavern at the Olde Pink House, but when Madison texted me that Jason was going to be at Anna's, I knew I had to go.

I never should have put that spell on Jason in the

first place. After all, when we first started going out, I didn't need any tricks. There I was, sitting on the MG bench one day, and this gorgeous boy just plops down next to me. "I'm Jason," he says. "And you must be the school goddess."

His dad's company was building a new golf course here or something, and he was already the best quarterback TRS had ever seen. I've had a lot of guys interested in me, but no one ever wooed me the way Jason did. From the moment he sat down next to me that day until our first kiss, six weeks later, I was the focus of his attention. There were gifts every week, notes every day, texts every hour. He was relentless, he was head over heels, he was committed—and I was flattered.

But as my grandmother says, "Easy woo, easy lose." I should have just cut him loose the second he started checking out other girls when they walked by, but I couldn't believe that this guy who'd been so into me, who'd said all those amazing things and spent so much time and money on me, could suddenly want anyone else. I refused to believe it, and so that's when I turned to Sina's tricks.

But now they're wearing off, and Jason has a wandering eye again, and I have to restore my charms or I'm going to be humiliated. I should probably just move on, but I love how cocky and how beautiful Jason is—how much better-looking he is than all the other guys in my class. The more my charm wears off, the crazier I am to make him like me again. I just wish he was into me the way Dexter is into Madison. If only things were *easy* between us. For now, though, I need to turn this around, and the first ingredient that the spell requires is a thread from Jason's shirt.

As my Prius crunches down the oyster-shell driveway to Anna's house (which actually has an official name: Secession), I'm charged with purpose. Going to Anna's plantation is like going back in time. Her dad's a lawyer, but his real passion is reenacting the Civil War, and this estate is his life's work. He's spent millions restoring Secession, packing it with loads of artifacts from the War Between the States, and basically anyone under the age of a hundred is forbidden to set foot inside — except Anna and her brother, Jackson, who have been trained from birth that running, touching, and talking loudly near the antiques are forbidden under penalty of death.

Needless to say, we are not allowed near the main house, but fortunately Anna's father built his kids their own little replica mansion. They call it the Dower House, and it's pretty impressive in its own right: regulation pool table, plasma screens, Wii, PS3...everything they could want, including that most important commodity of all — privacy.

I come around the side of Secession and stand in the shadows for a minute before plunging into battle.

Anna's been talking about her oyster roast for weeks, at the same time trying to make it sound like some casual little event she just threw together at the last minute. The widely anticipated Atlanta deejay is on the upstairs back porch spinning mashups, and from where I'm standing I can count at least three kegs. Poor Anna, she doesn't even drink; she just really, *really* wants to be popular. And actually, from the looks of it, she's succeeding. Kids are absolutely crammed in, and down by the river there are two huge fire pits full of glowing coals. They're so hot that the entire backyard feels like summer. Across the river I can see the lights of Savannah twinkling in the dark.

Normally this is when I'd tie on a last-minute Forget My Flaws charm, just to make sure I'm absolutely perfect, but I didn't remember to get any more blood root, so I have to settle for one last face check in my compact. Then I head into the mad crush of kids. Bushels of oysters are being dumped onto huge sheets of corrugated tin thrown over the fire pits, and wet burlap is tossed on top. Briny steam fills the night air. Jackson's college friends are scooping the steamed oysters off with shovels and dumping them down the middle of a long table made of plywood balanced on top of sawhorses. The table runs from one side of the yard to the other. It must be eighty feet long, and all around it kids are shucking oysters, drinking beer, passing fifths of liquor, throwing Frisbees, lighting

Swisher Sweets, and shouting to one another over the music. There is something almost pagan about the atmosphere. I don't know why, but it feels like a night that could end badly.

I keep my eyes peeled for Alex and put on my "party face"—slightly regal, friendly but not entirely approachable—but no one is familiar, and the few people I do recognize seem otherwise engaged. Then I notice most of the people from my class crowded around something. I make my way over to find a tight circle, and tap Anna's shoulder. She looks at me a bit sheepishly, then backs away to give me a view of the show.

"Oh. My. God," I breathe, horrified. "They're not—"

"They are!" Anna squeals.

It's Madison and Dexter and they're... *break-dancing.*

"Isn't it awesome? They are the *best* couple."

I am helpless to do anything but stare.

"Seriously," Anna babbles on, "it's so crazy. Last year, Madison would never have done anything this dorky. But ever since Alex came to school, it's like deep geek is *in.* It totally makes everything so much more fun, right? Like, more communist or something."

"I think you mean democratic."

"Same diff. Anyway, it's cool. Nice top! I'm gonna find Mary."

And Anna trips off, obviously thrilled about her

party. I sidle up to Madison, who has just finished her "robot."

"Um, Madison?"

"Oh, hi," she says, her sweaty glow of triumph edged with sheepishness. "Dex's idea. We watched *The LXD* last night, and then we stayed up till two a.m. teaching ourselves how to pop and lock from Jon Chu videos."

"That's great." I give the remark a casual drawl, trying not to sound flustered. "But you were supposed to come over last night and work on party stuff. I waited for you instead of going to see Jason."

"That's because you don't actually like the guy," Madison says.

"I—"

"You can't escape my eagle eyes. By the way, Alex hasn't shown up tonight."

"Have you talked to her?"

"No," Madison says. "I'm on your side, remember?"

"Thanks."

"So where *is* Jason, anyway?"

"I don't know," I say, looking around nervously.

"Howdy," Dex says, slinging his arm around Madison's shoulder. She kisses him, and suddenly it hits me like a thunderbolt: Everyone around me is in love, yet I'm not even close. I've never felt about Jason the way Thaddeus feels about Alex or the way Madison (Lord help her) feels about Dex. They all have relationships free of charms. Is that the answer? Have I screwed up the one thing that was good in my life? Maybe I can take another shot at Jason, but this time without the hoodoo.

"Hey, Hayester," Dexter says, using a nickname I abhor. "Isn't that your boyfriend?"

I look over to one end of the oyster table and see Jason holding court. In the firelight, he's truly breathtaking: six feet tall, shaved head, high cheekbones, flawless dark skin. Four girls from Savannah Day School are hanging on his every word, and one of them is standing suspiciously close to him. I can't blame any of them, and the sight makes me realize that now might not be the best time to try for a hoodoo-free relationship if I want to keep Jason.

"What are you going to do?" Madison asks.

"Kill them with kindness."

"Hey," Jason says as I appear over the shoulder of one of his new fans. "I didn't know you were coming out here tonight."

"Anna's one of my closest friends," I say. "I'm not about to skip her party."

"I just love oysters," one of the Savannah Day School girls says, obviously without a clue that *I* am going out with him. "They're *such* an aphrodisiac."

"You know what else is an aphrodisiac?" I ask.

"What?"

"Not getting punched by the girlfriend of the boy you're flirting with."

So much for the kindness. At least that scatters them. But instead of looking sheepish, Jason looks annoyed.

"Baby, that was cold," he complains.

I step up and give him one of my wettest, warmest kisses, just melting into his body to erase those girls from his memory. But it's not working. I can feel he's not into it. He's stiff, and he doesn't hold me as tightly as he normally does. I pull back, embarrassed.

"I just got jealous. You should be flattered."

"Cool," he says, distracted. "I'm going to get a beer. I'll be back in a minute."

"I'll come with."

"I'll bring you one, okay?" And then he pushes off through the crowd, leaving me stuck here all alone next to a fifty-gallon steel barrel full of fishy-smelling discarded oyster shells.

This is worse than I thought. Even if the hoodoo charm is wearing off, he's still seventeen. There shouldn't be anything on his mind other than this somewhat low-cut shirt I'm wearing. Do I really need a Come With Me, Boy to get him to pay any attention to me whatsoever? Surely I have some charms of my own. Don't I?

"Want me to shuck you an oyster?" some random guy says. "I hear they're an aphrodisiac."

A college friend of Jackson's is standing next to me in a pair of hipster eyeglasses and muttonchop side-burns. He's an inch shorter than I am, and he's holding an oyster in one hand.

"I'll hold it up to your lips, and you can suck it out of the shell," he says.

"Have we been introduced?"

"I'm Q-Ball."

"That's not actually a name."

"It's what I deejay under," he says. "You've probably heard of me. Here, open your mouth—this oyster's getting cold."

"Is this how you act with everyone?"

"Only girls like you," he grins. "I've got a weak-ness for curly hair."

Curly???

"Excuse me." I try to push past him and only suc-ceed in knocking his beer all over me.

"Hey!" he calls after me. "At least let me lick it off!"

I race for the Dower House, wait in line for the bathroom, and then lock the door behind me and stare into the mirror. I've augmented my looks so often—changed the color of my eyes, changed my hair, my skin, my teeth, my nails—that I barely remember what I used to look like. But one thing I do remember: my hair. It used to be frizzy, and in the Savannah humidity it was always sticking up like a wire brush.

My stepfather once called it "the Scrub Mop" and joked that he'd use my hair to clean the chimneys in our house. The first charm I ever laid on myself was to give me thick, straight hair. And now it's curly again?

No, no, no, no, *no.*

Yes. It's back. My hair is starting to frizz at the ends. It doesn't look bad yet, but I can see the Scrub Mop it's going to turn into if I don't get things under control. I study my face under the ugly light. My upper lip looks slightly different, and I run a finger over it: fuzz. My eyebrows look unruly. I look at my arms. I never have much in the way of arm hair, but now I see a few dark strands poking their heads up. There's even a dark hair growing out of one of my knuckles. I pluck it out, knowing it'll just be back by morning.

I slip out of the bathroom and creep around the edge of the party, sticking to the shadows as I make my way to the car. No time to worry about Jason. I'm falling apart. Why didn't I go looking for those stupid muckle bushes? I'll have to see if Sam or Sina will take pity on me and throw me some emergency charms on credit.

To get to the Buzzard's Roost, I have to drive way out into the country on Highway 21, where the houses get farther apart and the names of the churches get longer. I hate driving out here at night, with no streetlights and almost no houses.

I have 97.3 KISS FM playing, but suddenly the

radio starts to lose the station, and then all I get is static. Ahead of me the two-lane road vanishes into a tunnel of live oaks.

Suddenly, I see a man walking along the side of the road. My headlights pick him up as he puts out his thumb, and then he's gone. Weird. I didn't know anyone hitchhiked anymore.

And then, with a tiny *urp!* my Prius just cuts off. It's like a big hand has grabbed it and brought it to a stop. On the dashboard all the lights suddenly come on. I groan as my car glides to the side of the road and rolls off into the grass on the shoulder, and I flip on the hazard lights. They start flashing on and off with a reassuring clicking noise. I pull out my phone, but of course there's no 3G service out here.

I look in the rearview mirror. The big guy who was hitchhiking is still a ways down the road, still walking toward me. Maybe it's my lucky night and he's a mechanic or something. He's certainly big enough. Only the loud ticking of the hazard lights breaks the silence. The lights turn the trees yellow and then black.

"Hi," I call, getting out of the car when the big guy's about twenty yards away. He doesn't say anything, just keeps walking toward me. He's probably as scared of me as I am of him.

"Excuse me," I call as loudly as I can, when he gets closer. "Know anything about cars?"

He still doesn't answer. This is starting to make me seriously uneasy. Then he steps into the hazard lights, and I see that he has what looks like dirt over his eyes. The lights go yellow and then black and then yellow, and I see that his eyes aren't dirty; it's more like someone has drawn on his eyelids with a thick black marker...but wait. It's not a marker at all. *His eyes are sewn shut.*

He opens his mouth, and his teeth and tongue are black. He grins like he's hungry and then makes a hissing sound. I step back. He smells cold and...dead.

I stumble on my first step, then kick off my heels. My feet are freezing cold on the rough asphalt, but I'm running and putting some distance between myself and this *thing* on the road. I turn around and look back, and he's coming around my car, walking toward me in a completely unconcerned manner, like he knows no one is going to come help me.

I back away, keeping my eyes on him. No way am I letting him out of my sight. He's not coming any faster, just walking along, slowly, like he's in no hurry.

All right. I've got a half dozen protection charms I've been taught, but now I can't remember a single one of them. Let's see, there's the Pepper in Your Tears, which makes their eyes water, and the Thinking Man's Answer, which makes their thoughts as thick as syrup. But right this minute my brain is completely blank. I turn and run again.

The rough asphalt is tearing up my feet, and it's so cold that it feels like my bones are actually slapping the concrete with every step. But when I see what's ahead, I yelp with relief. I'm no senior Magnolia or hoodoo priestess, but I *do* know that if something dead is chasing you—be it a ghost, boo hag, or plat-eye—it can't come into a church. Even the place where a church has once been is considered sacred. So when I see the ruined foundations of Old Bethel, an AME church that burned in the sixties, I feel an indescribable surge of relief.

Expecting to see the large, shambling man far behind me, I slow and turn around. And yet he's right there. How did he get behind me so fast? He's just walking. The world lurches around me as it stops making sense, and I'm frozen, like a deer in the headlights. A long whine of fear stretches out of my throat, and my legs go numb. He grins again. That does it.

With everything I have, I turn and run faster, pumping my legs, running so hard my chest aches. Acorns on the ground cut my feet; I can actually feel my skin tearing, can feel the blood. Still, I don't stop until I'm over that ruined wall. Only then do I dare to look back.

He's there, of course. So close. And he's horrible. Furious. He tries to move forward but literally can't. After two more attempts, he lets out the worst, most guttural scream I've ever heard. This is what hell would sound like if it were a person.

I pray he's going to stop now, but no. He keeps bellowing, making his awful, furious, yawping howl, turning my blood to ice. I put my head down on my knees and squeeze my eyes shut so hard I see spots. *Please please please*, I chant. *Please please please.* For now, the words are all I know. All I remember.

When I open my eyes again, the sky is pink. I must have fallen asleep. I lift my head slowly. The Thing is gone, as far as I can see.

"Is she a homeless?"

I'm stiff, cold, sore, and covered in bruises. I feel like someone's kicked me down the stairs. But above me is the most beautiful little boy I've ever seen. Just the fact that he's alive makes him beautiful. Behind him is his dad, a big guy wearing a red plaid shirt.

"You okay, miss?" the dad asks. He's got a camera around his neck, and I notice his son is holding a pair of binoculars as big as he is.

"I'm fine," I say, sitting up. Trying to sound normal and not like some scary freak. "Bird-watching?"

"Well, yes. Listen, do you want us to call an ambulance or something? Did someone hurt you?"

"No, no, no. I'm good."

I force myself to get up. My body screams in agony. I stretch and instantly feel worse and better at the same time. They're both staring at me, so I figure I need to say something by way of explanation. "I was just, um, falling asleep while I was driving, and I figured it was safer if I pulled over to catch a nap."

"In a ruined church?"

"It's scenic. Do you have the time?"

"Ten forty," the man says, and adrenaline surges through my body. *The Magnolia meeting.* I'm already late.

"Thanks!" I call over my shoulder. "Enjoy your bird-watching."

I run, or rather limp, back up the road to my car. The hazard lights aren't flashing anymore—not a good sign. I don't have time for a dead battery. I slide behind the wheel, press the ignition button, and start my mantra again: *Please, please, please.*

It actually starts.

12

"Sina!" Sam bursts into the cottage, slamming the door open so hard the walls shake. Sina, still exhausted from the night before, opens one eye to look at him.

"Mornin'," she says. "What, I slept through breakfast?"

"Don't play with me. What the hell have you been doing with Alex the past couple of days?" He looks around the room, still wrecked from one end to the other by William Long's tantrum. "What happened in here?"

"Shouldn't we ask the real question?" Sina says, rolling over on her stomach and lifting her chest and shoulders up like a sphinx. "Why the hell do you care?"

Sam gives her an angry look and starts opening and closing the cabinets. Finally he finds what he's looking for: dried saw grass. He takes a pinch and puts it between his lip and cheek in order to calm his nerves.

"She's our client," he says.

"So are all the Magnolias. Hayes Anderson. Mary Oglethorpe. You don't care about what they're doin'."

"I am concerned for each and every one of them according to their needs," he says. "And right now, I have a feeling you were showing Alex how to break one of The Three."

"If you had proof, you wouldn't be asking."

"This is not the time for you to start playing cute," Sam says. "I'll drag Doc into this if I have to."

"All right, it was a Three problem. But I was just helping. Trying to fix things already broken. But *I* didn't break them."

"What do you mean?"

"Girl was rooted. All I did was pull the Gray Man out of her."

Sam sits down in Sina's carved mahogany chair and puts his head in his hands. "Do you know what you've done?"

"I rescued your precious Alexandria Lee from the Gray Man. You should be bringin' me breakfast in bed."

"Sina, where do you think the Gray Man went? To Piggly Wiggly, where it's half-price Saturdays? You think he's out doing a little shopping?"

"Not my problem," Sina says, rising and taking down the broom from its place over the door. She starts sweeping up the broken glass in her kitchen.

"It is your problem, and it's the biggest problem you ever had. They found a boy dead last night. Right up the road."

Sina pauses for a moment, then continues to sweep. "Kids die all the time. Probably drunk."

"He was at a party, sure. Everyone saw him leave, but then he had some engine trouble down past the Old Bethel Church. They found his car over on Skitter's Lane. The boy was on the shoulder of the road, every bone in his body fractured."

"Well—"

"Would you like to know what else, Sina? His eyes were missing. They're saying it was a hit-and-run, but we both know what it is."

Sina sweeps furiously. "A hit-and-run."

"The Gray Man. It's the Gray Man you cut loose. You've got to put them down when you're done. You know that!"

"You think I had time?" Sina snaps. "I was making sure he didn't rip your little Alex open."

"You're supposed to be the adult," Sam yells back, his voice rising. "You're not supposed to let yourself get flustered by a Gray Man or some sixteen-year-old child. We all know you meddle with things that are bigger than all of us put together, and we all know that you go places everyone else is too smart to venture. Until now, you've always been responsible about it. You've always been careful, so no one's ever reined you in. Not anymore. It's time Doc clipped your wings."

"It was a bad one, Sam," Sina says quietly. She sits on the couch, shaken by the memory. "Nastiest I've ever seen. I think he was a killer from around these parts a long time ago...."

"Name?"

"William Long."

"Worst there is, Sina," he says. "Madame Laveau herself ensured that one upon us. He was Savannah's blockade-runner version of Jack the Ripper."

"Likes cake."

"Likes *death*. He killed thousands of slaves from boats he raided. Stole their talismans and charms, then tossed them overboard. He rules the In Between, Sina. And you let him loose."

"You wanted him to hurt Alex?" Sina spits.

Sam runs his hand through his hair. "You know we have to tell Doc," Sam says. "Cops are going to be looking around, asking questions. At least if we tell Doc to his face, he won't be as angry as if he figures it out on his own."

"We do need to talk to Doc," Sina says. "But not about this."

"What about?"

"Someone wanted the Gray Man to *kill* that girl," Sina says. "It might even be the same person who killed her mother."

"What?"

"How else you think Louisa Lee died?" Sina says. "Why do you think she died the second she put down the buzzard's rock? Coincidence? Someone took that charm away from her, then murdered her. And I think it's the same person who put the Gray Man on Alex."

"It wasn't you, was it?" Sam asks, suddenly scared of the answer.

"Would I be telling you if it was? Before he left, the Gray Man described who called him up and set him on that girl."

"Who?"

"He wasn't the best conversationalist, but funny thing—he sure did describe Miss Lee to a T."

"That's impossible," Sam says quickly.

Sina rolls her eyes in exasperation. "Naturally. You know everything."

"I know that Miss Lee wouldn't have rooted her own granddaughter."

"Let's go to Doc together because this is something he needs to know," Sina says. "The Magnolias are breaking out The Three. Miss Lee raised up a Gray Man; she set him on her daughter and then again on her granddaughter. That's two of The Three right there. All she hasn't done is look into the future and, for all we know, she's doing that every other Saturday. The woman's nuts. It's time we got Doc to cut her off."

"You're wrong," Sam says, getting up and pacing. "I know you want the Magnolias taken down a peg, but you couldn't be more wrong about this."

"Why?"

Sam rubs his palms together. "I shouldn't tell you this."

"You already made up your mind to spill, so stop beating around the bush."

"Miss Lee hired me to keep Louisa safe. To keep her from passing over. She didn't kill her; she's been trying to keep her here. She can't bear to be without her."

With a snap, Sina uncoils herself from the sofa. "You tied her down to the In Between, didn't you?"

"Yeah."

Sina shakes her head in disbelief. "I knew you loved her, but enough to keep her trapped in a place like that? You didn't do it for Miss Lee, brother. You did it for *you*."

"She was taken!" he shouts. "We *all* know it."

"And it might have been by her own mother!" Sina shouts back. "Wake up! Louisa has always had you dancing on her string, and now that she's gone you've just gone and passed the leash over to her mama. You love-drunk fool, you've gone behind Doc's back, you've helped Miss Lee break The Three, and I'm out here cleaning up your mess!"

"Dorothy Lee didn't call up the Gray Man," Sam says. "Get that through your skull."

"You're in way deeper than I am, brother, and you're sinking fast."

"Then we have to tell Doc everything," Sam says, resigned. He stares glumly at the floor.

Sina looks at him for a moment. She's always been quick on her feet, and this is the first time all morning she's felt like the advantage is hers again. She might even come out ahead.

"No, Sam," she says. "We can clean this up, and no one will be the wiser. I'll find the Gray Man. You need to get rid of Louisa Lee. Set the woman free."

"I can't."

"All right," Sina says, pretending to sigh. "All right, then. Let her stay. You want to trap the woman you love in the In Between, that's none of my business. But the anniversary of her death is coming up fast. If you're not going to give her a second burial, then at least let her out of that room."

"What room?" Sam says sharply.

Sina tries to cover her slip.

"I assume she's in her mama's house," she says.

"Trapped upstairs or something. Where else would she be?"

Sam looks at her from the corner of his eyes for a moment. "You think you're so smart," he says. "And I almost bought your act. But you've known about Louisa all along, haven't you? What are you playing at, Sina?"

"I'm not playing, I'm trying to help my brother, who's too dumb to think straight. So should we go up to Doc's and tell him what's going on? Because if so, you're going to have to give me a few minutes to do my hair. I'm not going to get reamed by that old Buzzard looking like I just woke up."

"You win, Sina," Sam says. "For now, consider we're at a stalemate. You find the Gray Man, and I'll figure out what to do about Louisa Lee. And let's leave Doc out of this for the time being."

"If that's how you want it," Sina says.

"It's how *you* want it," Sam says, and he leaves.

Sina sits down and sighs. She pulls out her cell phone and dials Alex's number. It is going to take everything she has to keep Sam from releasing Louisa Lee before her second burial. And if Sam lets that woman free, then Sina's deal with Alex is off. It's going to take some careful planning, and maybe even some outside help, to make sure that doesn't happen.

13

Hayes

Having spent the night in an old, ruined church, cornered by some kind of insane ghost, I look worse than bad. I look downright scary. And as a result of not making it to Sina's last night, my hair is as wild as a Brillo pad, I've broken out from stress, and my skin looks pale—and not in a pretty porcelain way. I know that going to the Magnolia meeting is a very, very bad idea, especially in this condition, but I don't have a choice.

Of course, I hit traffic, and by the time it clears,

there's no way I can make it to my house and then to 404 Habersham. Fortunately, a real lady is always prepared for any crisis, and so I pull over at a gas station and grab my emergency "pretty" bag out of the trunk. All right—after five minutes in the bathroom with some wet wipes, my makeup, and a clean, pressed top, I look almost human again.

I make it to Magnolia headquarters at 11:20, which means I'm coming in after Miss Lee—a true sin, even for the granddaughter of one of the Senior Four. I just pray that they all got caught up in socializing and didn't actually sit down for the meeting yet. But when I get to the closed upstairs door, I realize that I'm going to have no such luck.

I tiptoe in, hoping to slip unnoticed into a chair along the wall, but the moment I enter the room, everything stops. My grandmother is in the middle of a sentence, Dorothy Lee and Alex sit across the table staring at me, and Khaki Pettit is there with Madison, both their mouths hanging open.

"Well, isn't this something," Dorothy Lee finally says.

"We were just discussing a change of venue for the fund-raiser," my grandmother says grimly. "Do you have that list of ticket buyers, Hayes?"

"The what?"

"The list of people who have bought tickets. The one we spoke about yesterday."

My heart sinks.

"I forgot...."

My grandmother sighs hopelessly.

"Do we need to adjourn until tomorrow?" Dorothy Lee asks.

Everyone's staring at me. My grandmother comes over and gives me a hug. I'm about to cry out of gratitude, but then she hisses in my ear, "Stop embarrassing me."

She guides me to a seat.

"We actually *have* sold a lot of tickets," Alex says. "Close to a hundred."

"Well!" my grandmother says to her, looking over at me as if I have leprosy. "Isn't that an accomplishment? But I don't suppose you brought a list either?"

"Actually, I did," Alex says, pulling out some papers and sliding them across the table. I can tell that Dorothy Lee is beaming on the inside.

"We should probably consider a bigger venue," Alex says. "Savannah Station or something. With the tickets I sold, we're already at capacity. I don't think anyone anticipated this kind of response."

"I don't know," I say stupidly. "I've only sold two tickets. I don't think that many people actually want to go."

"Hayes," Alex says patiently. "I'm sure you could sell more...if you *tried*."

Everyone's staring at me with pity. I can't stand it

anymore. I know I look terrible—I can see my thoroughly hideous reflection in a mirror across the room—but I can't let them just sit there and think I'm willingly walking around looking like some kind of living corpse.

"I was *attacked* last night," I cry.

"Pardon?" Dorothy Lee says.

"She's just worked up," my grandmother stage-whispers. "Let's move on.'..."

"It was a big fat guy. A gray ghost or something. It came after me."

Alex leans forward, looking alarmed.

"My car broke down and I thought he was a person who might help me. Then I saw that he was some kind of monster with his eyes sewn shut, and I ran into Old Bethel AME, where he couldn't get me."

No one says anything, so I keep going. "Maybe because it's holy ground still, or something like that? And this morning he was gone and I don't know why he came after me but I think it's really serious. I don't know if we should have this party. Maybe we should cancel it?"

There's a silence so thick that you could cut it with a knife and serve it up on the good china with ice cream. Finally:

"Hayes," my grandmother says. "What on earth are you babbling about? And why do you smell like a brewery?"

146

I didn't have a fresh pair of jeans in the bag, and despite my cleanup attempt and a new shirt, the spilled beer from last night is starting to stink in the warm air.

"What is going on?" Dorothy Lee asks. "Should we be worried?"

"No, it's true," I babble. "Go ask Sina. Or Doc Buzzard. I bet they know about it. You're crazy to have this event while he's out there."

"Grandmother, I think she just needs a rest," Alex says quickly.

"But—"

"There was a party last night," Alex says, leaning confidentially toward the Senior Four. "Way out at Secession. A lot of the kids were probably drunk, or even worse. And there's been a lot of pressure on Hayes at school."

I can't believe she's doing this.

"I was *not* drunk. I left that party early to . . . run an errand, and I am not lying, and it is not stress."

"Hayes," Madison whispers, grabbing my arm. "Seriously. You need to chill."

"I can handle organizing the party on my own," Alex says. "Hayes seems a little off today, but this party will definitely happen in a big way. We just need a bigger venue."

"Listen to me!" I shout, and even I'm surprised at myself. "I saw this . . . thing last night. It's real!"

Everyone looks toward my grandmother.

"Hayes," she says. "I think you should go home.

You look terrible, and you sound like a cuckoo bird. Sleep it off and I'll see you tomorrow."

"But I'm part of the party *committee*," I whimper. "It's my job as a Magnolia."

"Not anymore."

"There's nothing wrong with me!"

"There is something wrong with you!" my grandmother snaps. "Your display of rudeness. Now please leave so that we can go about our business."

I know better than to fight, and so, defeated, I walk out the door. After I close it behind me, I listen for a minute. The first voice I hear is, of course, Alex's.

"So, what's the next step?" she asks eagerly.

I walk downstairs and call Jason. After one ring it goes to voice mail—he's screening his calls. I shuffle outside and dive into my car, where I finally let myself cry.

14

Alex

Okay. I know throwing Hayes under the Magnolia
bus was bad. Actually, it was worse than bad: It was
evil. And evil is how I felt after I said those things and
made her look so crazy in front of everyone. After I
fed her to the wolves, I saw her face, and she looked
exactly like she did the day her grandmother tore into
her in front of 404 Habersham. It wasn't even the Gray
Man talking back there in the meeting—Sina did her
job. I'm suffering from no outside influences. The

person who did that to Hayes was me, speaking of my own free will. And what I did was just wrong.

But I'm not sorry. Hayes was about to give the Magnolias a very good reason to cancel the Louisa Lee Memorial Greenhouse Gala, and that would have messed up all my plans. Because if the Magnolias believe her about the Gray Man being on the loose, they'll probably realize that Sina had something to do with it. And I can't let my grandmother figure out that Sina was working with me—that's the last thing that can happen.

But right now I have a much bigger problem. It sounds as though the Gray Man found another prey: Hayes. Even after I've practically killed myself keeping him away from my friends. How am I going to raise my mother and keep Hayes safe? Even if I manage to master the darkest hoodoo secrets, I'm getting spread a little thin.

Of course, right now I'm in way more danger than the Gray Man ever put me in. Madison's called me three times—no doubt out for my blood.

She's not in the school parking lot, or out front, but the second I set foot in the breezeway, I feel her china-blue gaze hit me like a pair of laser beams. I look up and there she is across the lawn, looking truly spectacular in an aquamarine silk top, skinny jeans, and gorgeous Italian boots. She always looks like she's headed to a glossy magazine shoot, instead of wading through trig like the rest of us. She comes across the lawn with the swagger of a Power Ranger, then puts my arm in the steel clamp of death and steers me toward the MG bench.

As soon as the other girls see us coming, they scatter like a flock of seagulls. Madison plops me down roughly, crosses her arms, and narrows her eyes at me.

"What are you?" she says. "An emotional abuser? Do I need to call a hotline? Because I have to assume this is how you get your sick kicks: publicly humiliating the one person who's been nice to you the entire time you've been here."

I have to tread carefully. Madison is sharper than Hayes about this kind of thing. Harder to lie to.

"All I can say is that you don't understand the circumstances."

"No? That's funny coming from the girl who has her head so far up her grandmother's butt that she's wearing her like a hat. Let me paint you a word picture of the circumstances: Hayes is falling apart. Jason's flaking, and her grades are tanking. Did you really have to take over this stupid party when it's the one thing she's into right now?"

"She wanted to cancel it."

"Postponement! Because there's a friggin' blood-thirsty monster thing on the loose!"

"The Gray Man doesn't drink blood, Mad. Quit reading those vampire books."

"*Why* did you do that to her, you little backstabber?"

"I didn't have a choice," I protest. "The party, has to be on the anniversary of my mother's death; otherwise, what's the point? The date has significance."

"N00b, you're the one who was all up in arms about your mother's death birthday in the first place," Madison hisses. "What is with you?"

"Sorry to interrupt," Anna says triumphantly, flouncing up to us in a truly squint-worthy neon-pink sweater dress. "Just wanted to tell Alex I'm sorry."

"About what?"

"About your boyfriend. It's so awful."

"My boyfriend?" My heart literally stops. I jerk my head around, scanning the lawn for the beautiful boy with the blond hair. Where is Thaddeus? Madison must be thinking the same thing.

"Yeah. Owen."

"Ohhhhhh." I put my hand on my chest and sink back down on the bench. "Is he okay?"

"No," Madison says quietly. "He's not."

"What?"

Anna leans in a bit too eagerly. "I hate to be the one to tell you. But it's better you find out from a friend. I guess he parked on Alligator Road, and everyone's saying he threw himself in front of a truck or whatever." She shakes her head as if having a solemn moment, and then brightens and looks at me curiously. "Did y'all get into a fight?"

"No," I say, feeling sick.

"The weirdest thing was that his eyes were pecked out by birds or something. Alex, you must be really broken up."

"I'm sad, yeah," I say truthfully. "But, Anna, I hardly knew the guy."

"Not what *I* heard," Anna says. "Owen Bailey told *everyone* what you guys did at the deer stand, Alex. Seems a little cheap to deny it now."

I blink, trying to take all this in. I can't believe Owen died this way. He wasn't my favorite, but just thinking about it makes me feel faint. Did the Gray Man possess him right away? Take over his body? I try to imagine what he must have been thinking right before he died. . . . Well, unfortunately I suspect I know exactly what he was thinking: that death was better than suffering with this monster inside.

"Gross, Anna," Madison says, bringing me back to the present. "No one actually fools around on a deer stand. Think about it. The whole point is to be quiet and not scare the animals. Now shoo. The grown-ups are talking."

"Whatever." Anna sniffs, then saunters away.

"Thanks," I say to Madison, grateful for the save.

"The notion that you would make out with Owen

Bailey—God rest his soul—makes all of us MGs look bad. But it doesn't change the fact that you are seriously on my list. There will be a reckoning, and it will be—"

Suddenly, there's a crackle overhead. *"Students, due to tragic circumstances, there will be an emergency community meeting in the auditorium. Please gather there at the next bell for a special announcement. Attendance is mandatory."*

And then the bell rings.

"Well, that'll be the Please-Pray-for-Owen assembly," Madison says. "Poor guy. He didn't deserve this kind of thing. I feel bad for his family."

"Yeah...well. I'll see you later."

I turn and start walking in the opposite direction from the auditorium.

"Wait. You're cutting?" Madison asks.

"I've got things to do."

"Like figuring out how you're going to make it up to Hayes?"

"Yeah," I say, but my mind is already buzzing. God, did *I* kill Owen? Is the monster going to return and kill me next? And, most important, *where is the Gray Man now*? He could be coming back to school right this second. I've never had a panic attack before, but I think I'm having one now. Someone grabs my shoulder.

"Look," Madison says, standing way too close for comfort. "I don't know what's up with you, but if something's gone wrong, you need to tell me."

"I can't."

"Why?"

"I mean, nothing's wrong. Look, I forgot to tell the florist to keep Gerber daisies out of the arrangements. My grandmother will totally hurl if the colors are too bright in the greenhouse—it being a memorial and all. So I'll catch you later, okay?"

"Yeah," Madison says, eyeing me suspiciously. "Okay."

I hurry across the lawn so quickly I trip over the root of an oak tree. Not bothering to look back to see if Madison noticed, I jog to the parking lot. I'm the only one who can put this thing to rest now. It's already too late for Owen. But I'd rather go to hell—literally—than have anyone else around me die.

Everyone at TRS is heading to the assembly. There'll probably be a policeman talking about what happened, a bit of grief counseling, maybe a lecture on drunk driving from Constance. Afterward, they'll give everyone the day off, at which point the kids will burst from the doors as if released from a huge pressure chamber, heading for Massy's or Pinkie's or some other place that'll serve them beer. Which means I probably have about forty-five minutes to get what I need before anyone gets home.

A couple of kids look at me curiously as I start the car, but I hope, given my "relationship" with Owen, they'll just think I'm grieving. I slide out of the parking lot as quietly as I can, get safely through the TRS gates, then stand on the gas pedal and drive like a bat out of hell to the Andersons' house. Careful to park a block away, I run into the back of their garden, praying that no one's there.

I fish the key out from underneath the flowerpot and let myself in. No cars are in the driveway, so I hope that means the house is empty, but if Ellie or Hayes's stepfather is around, I'm just going to have to be quiet. The dog pads into the kitchen, and I feed him a strip of bacon from the fridge. Then, taking the servants' stairs in the back, I tiptoe as quietly as a cat into Hayes's perfectly decorated pink-and-gold room.

Which is, oddly, a mess. Clothes are all over the floor, and makeup is strewn across the dresser, staining the white wood brown and pink. Even her spell box is open and disorganized, as if Hayes were desperately trying to put together some spells. My heart beats faster. What's really going on with my friend?

Although Hayes said the rock was in her spell box, it's not. Crap. It could be anywhere in this pigsty. I rifle through her jewelry box, look through her drawers. Nothing. Under the bed, on top of the closet. No, no, no. I start to get more frantic as time ticks away. I think I hear something toward the front of the house. Was it a door opening? Was that someone coming up the front stairs? I have to hurry.

One last shot, as stupid as it seems. What is Hayes

obsessed with? France. I turn to her bookshelf, zeroing in on the French books. Colette, Hugo, *Fodor's Guide to Paris*. I dump the books out, and behind them, on the back of the shelf, is the necklace that will enable me to beat this monster forever and keep us all safe.

The rock is hanging from a nail. Carefully, I take it down and look at it. It's amazing that such an unassuming piece of jewelry has so much power. As I rub the twine in my fingers, I'm overwhelmed with memories of my mom. Is some of her aura still on the fibers? Her cells? I'm tempted to just fasten it around my neck, but if Hayes notices it's gone, hell will break loose. I can't have that right now. I'll give it back to her as soon as I can, but for now I've got to use it to protect us all.

I carefully take the stone out of its loose twine setting and slip it into my purse, and then from her spell box I take a smooth stone about the same size and shape, slide it into the buzzard stone's place, and hang the necklace up again. Unless you looked closely, you wouldn't be able to tell the difference. I slip the naked buzzard's rock into my pocket and back out of the room. It looks like I was never here. I run as fast as I can down the servants' stairs…straight into Thaddeus, who proceeds to scream at the top of his lungs and spill some kind of green smoothie all over me.

"Jesus!"

"Oh my God!" I yell, falling backward onto the step.

157

"Alex! You scared the hell out of me!" He looks at my shirt and laughs in spite of himself. "Sorry."

"What is this? It smells disgusting."

"Spinach and spirulina. It's a lacrosse thing."

"Nice."

"Anyway, what the hell are you doing here?"

"Ummm…" Think fast, Alex. Faster. *Faster!* "I — was seeing if Hayes was home."

"She's at school. At the assembly. But I was a little shaken up, so…" We look at each other. He's perfect, as ever. Pressed khakis, gray V-neck sweater, a snowy white button-down shirt beneath.

"Right. School. Of course. But I thought she might be here."

"They have magical devices for asking her personally, you know. I'm surprised the Magnolias haven't taught you about them yet. They're called cell phones. People carry them in their pockets and —"

"I wanted to make sure she was okay. I noticed she's been off lately."

Thaddeus looks at me carefully. He's only one step away. He doesn't move, and I don't either.

"She's not the only one," he says. "I've been worried about you."

"Thaddeus, we talked about this. I —"

Suddenly, I can't talk anymore. Not because I don't want to, but because I've been crushed into his chest. He pulls me, hard, into him and holds me. I want to pull away, but it's nice, and I breathe in the scent of him through his soft cashmere sweater. This is exactly what I want him to do. Exactly. I want him to take over and take care of me and not let me go.

But then I think I smell something dead, and I go cold. The Gray Man could be coming any minute. What if he had gotten Thaddeus instead of Owen? How could I live with myself if I'd gotten Thad killed?

I struggle to get away from him. But he's stronger than I am, and he's not budging.

"Let me go," I say into the wool.

"No."

For a moment I stop moving. There's so much I want to tell him. How scared I am. How much I hate myself for hurting him. For hurting everyone. How all I want is for everything to be okay.

"Tell me what's going on, Alex."

I'm scared to move. Scared to breathe.

"I *know* this isn't you."

I shake my head.

"Come on, you little nut." He squeezes me harder. "If you can't tell me what's going on, then who can you tell? Don't you know that I love you?"

I inhale sharply. My mind spins. *Wait.*

"You *do*?"

"What? I can't hear you down there."

"You do?" I whisper, looking up. "How can you? All I do is hurt you. All the time."

Thaddeus manages to grin, and he pulls me so close to his body I can feel everything—his chest, his stomach, his buttons, everything. "Technically, you're not hurting me right *now*."

"Well…"

And then he kisses me. And even though I've spent the last weeks trying to block out just how amazing it is to be kissed by a beautiful boy who you love and who loves you back, I realize now that I'll never be able to. The body doesn't forget these things. I'll remember this when I'm old—I know I will. I'll think of this kiss right before I die.

Suddenly, we hear the front door open. The spell is broken, and he pulls away.

"I've—"

"Gotta go. I get it." I feel the emptiness where his body was. "Someday you'll tell me what's going on, Alex."

I look at him for a long time. Again, I'm afraid to nod. Any encouragement could be fatal. But I'm too tired to protest. Instead, I slip past him as quietly as I can and, with the buzzard's rock burning a hole in my pocket, make my way out the door.

15

Hayes

Over the next two weeks, the River School seems to go crazy. I mean, we're all sad about Owen. He wasn't my favorite person, but we all feel horrible for his mother and father. But TRS is taking this thing a little too far. Terrified of being sued or somehow found responsible for Owen's presumed suicide, the school has brought in grief counselors, loss therapists, even someone called a "death coach." In one class I had to put numbered tennis balls into a bucket, and in another we all blew bicycle horns. I have no idea what any of it had to do with Owen, but Mr. Bailey did donate a nice new plaque:

OWEN BAILEY
"HE INSPIRED US TO FLY HIGHER."

Having someone our own age die — even if he did make kissing noises at the girls when we walked past him in the hall — has shaken us all up. We all still talk about him at lunch, trying to remember funny things he said. I managed to remember that he once drew a cartoon of Miss Taylor calling her "peg leg." He got a detention for that drawing back in the day, but now we've framed it and hung it up in the front hallway. I don't know. Death does funny things to people.

When life gets chaotic and strange, I always fall back on the code of behavior that my grandmother taught me. See, a lot of people make fun of the Magnolia League for sticking to our Southern traditions. They think we're too old-fashioned. But ask Mrs. Bailey. I think she could care less about the River School's moment of silence, but thanks to the Magnolias' casserole chain, she has something in the fridge to offer the countless people who stop by in her time of loss. There's a lot to be said for knowing the right thing to do and then simply doing it.

So today I'm trying to be graceful among the less so, watching Dexter eat my sushi for me (not hungry — and also, because the rest of my charms have been fading, I'm scared of a Canary malfunction) while I listen to everyone jabber away about school, Owen, and life and death.

"Hayes! You need your meds?"

I look up at Madison, who's snapping her fingers in front of my face. Everyone is staring at me.

"I'm sorry," I say, buying time for a recovery and return volley. "I was just so tired of hearing about Owen. He seems to be much more popular in death than in life."

"Ouch-ola," Dexter says.

"You're right. I'm sorry. I'm under a lot of stress."

"Hey," Madison says. "There's your former friend. Wanna talk to her?"

Alex is making her way across the lawn at a rapid clip. Since Owen died, she's been keeping to herself even more than usual. Unfortunately, she's also been looking extremely well. Her cheeks are pink, her eyes are gleaming—it's as if she's got a whole new sense of purpose.

"No."

Suddenly, something occurs to me. Why is everything in my life going so badly...when everything in her life seems to be going so well? How into the hoodoo is she? After all, my grandmother tried to steal Miss Dorothy's handkerchief to give her the what for. Has Alex learned her tricks? Has Alex been going through my things and rooting *me*?

I shoot up, scattering napkins on the ground.

"Hey, watch it!" Dex says.

"I'm sorry," I say, flustered. "It turns out I have something to do."

"Shop?" Madison says.

"Yes," I toss back over my shoulder. "In my own room."

I know it's completely out of character for me to cut school, but I need to follow this hunch. The first thing I do when I get home is carefully check and make sure there's no powder, goofer dirt, or anything else scattered on the threshold. Foot-track magic is exactly the kind of sneaky ambush Alex would try, laying some pattern in dust or powder over a place I'll walk so I'll be forced to absorb it through the soles of my shoes. Then I sniff all my shoes to make sure no deer's-tongue has been rubbed on them to put a Talk Stopper spell on me. They all smell fine.

There are hundreds of hiding places in my room where she could have put a conjure bag or written a sigil or tucked away a tiny vial of oil or a small bundle of herbs tied with a strand of my hair.

Okay, calm down, Hayes. You're being paranoid. You have no proof Alex did anything.

I take three deep breaths, and then my world tips upside down. *Someone has moved my Paris books.*

Only I would know, of course. But I prefer my Chéri books after the Claudine series. And someone (who obviously doesn't know French) has put them back in exactly the wrong order. It stands out like a glowing coal.

But when I take a closer look, everything seems okay. Nothing is amiss. The buzzard's rock necklace is still there behind a couple of novels.

I pull out a vial of Revealing Oil and rub it on the bookshelf, spreading a thin layer of it down the sides of the box, where someone might have touched it. Then I write the names of everyone in my family on scraps of paper and scatter them. They all land facedown. I write the names of Madison and Dexter and Alex on scraps of paper and let them fall.

I open my eyes. Only one name lands faceup: *Alex*. She's been in my room.

I've never been so scared before. I know Alex wants to undermine me in front of the Magnolias, but her sneaking into my room can only mean one thing. I'm not paranoid. She really is out to get me.

I check under my bed for a conjure bag, look in my closets for a hoodoo bundle or a bottle spell working against me. There's nothing, but that doesn't mean she hasn't hidden something somewhere in this room. I lift my mattress to see if she's working chalk mark magic on me. I pull all my clothes out of my closet—she could have sewn a paper talisman in a seam of my gym clothes. Then I realize she could have hidden something behind my books. I pull them all off the shelves, but there's nothing there. I can't stop. She hid something in here. Somewhere. I know it. *I have to find it.*

"What in the world?"

I freeze and see my grandmother standing in the doorway.

"Why on *earth* are you not at school?"

"I . . . I . . . I need help."

"I'll drink to that," my grandmother answers, then turns her head and calls out, "Ellie! What is wrong with your girl?"

Your girl? She's never called me that before. It's always "*my* granddaughter" with her.

"N-no, Grandmother, please," I stammer. "There's something in my room. You have to help me."

"My God, Hayes," Mom says, arriving in the door and staring at the mess. "What have you done to your things?"

I try to see this from their point of view. Everything is pulled off my shelves, my clothes are all over the floor, pictures are thrown all over the place, most of them torn out of their frames so I could check them thoroughly. I even dumped my garbage can out on the floor to make sure there was no sigil chalked on the bottom. It literally looks like a bomb went off.

"I think Alex put a root on me. You've got to help me find it."

"Put a root on you? Hayes, are you feeling all right?" my grandmother asks. "I highly doubt you are in possession of your wits at this time if you're talking like this. Much as I hate to say it."

"You've been distracted all month," my mother says. "It's that party; it's too much for you. And really, honey, you can't just skip school like this."

"Well, *I* came by to ask what's happening with the deposit for the caterers," my grandmother says to my mom. "Then I hear all this banging and whatnot, and I come upstairs to find your daughter standing here in this mess."

"It's Alex," I protest. "She did this!"

"Alex did this?" my grandmother asks skeptically.

"Yes!"

"So is *Alex* the one who didn't give a deposit to the caterers?"

"What?" I feel my stomach sinking.

"I asked your mother to make sure the caterers for the memorial-fund event got their deposit by yesterday, which was the deadline. She told me she'd have you drop off the check. So where is it?"

Oh my God. My purse.

"I meant to do it—"

"*Meant to* doesn't get anything done. I see that the check has not been cashed, so I call Savannah Caterers to go over hors d'oeuvres this morning, and they tell me they never received it. Can you imagine how mortified I was? Not only that, but they went and took a job working a wedding for Jo Shaw's boy on the night of the memorial-fund gala. That boy doesn't have the sense God gave a pig, and he doesn't deserve to eat their pecan sandies, but there you are. The whole thing is off." She shakes her head. "It was a simple thing, Hayes. One simple thing, and you couldn't handle it."

"Surely you can call and speak to Marshal Remember over there," my mother says.

"Of course I can," my grandmother says. "There's no question that I'll find someone who can fix this, but I'll be doing it on my own because you two are just pathetic. Now, before I say something I'll regret, I am going to brew some Swamp Brew for Hayes that you can give her, Ellie, and then I am going to try to clean up your mistakes."

I can't help crying, but my grandmother's face is closed off and cold. She and my mother leave, bickering all the way down the stairs. I flop down on my bed in the middle of my ruined room, and I stay there for the rest of the day. After a while I start picking up and reorganizing, trying to make things look like I didn't go on a rampage. I read somewhere that happiness starts with a clean room. I've never been this miserable, so I hope tidiness will help.

After a few hours, I hear Thaddeus open and close the front door. He must have heard about my run-in with my grandmother, because instead of his customary refrigerator safari, he comes straight up the stairs to my room.

"I'm fine," I reassure him before he can say anything.

"I know," he says, looking confused. "But I need to talk to you. Something's wrong with Alex."

"Not interested. Don't want to hear it."

He ignores me and sits at my desk.

"Look, I know it's wrong, but I've been following her."

"What? Get over her, Thaddeus. She clearly doesn't want you around anymore."

"I'm not so sure about that."

I shake my head. What did she put on him? Even Jason, at the height of the love charm's influence, wasn't as pathetic as this.

"She's been going out to the Roost. A lot. I think she's trying to do something with Sina."

"She's trying to put a root on me, I'm sure."

"I don't think so. She was crying the other day in her car. I think there's really something wrong."

"So what?"

"So she might be in danger."

"Thaddeus, if anything has been made perfectly clear to me recently, it's that Alex Lee can take care of herself."

"She's your friend, Hayes. And she needs your help."

"She's not my friend, actually. Now get out of my room before I get out the bull fertility spray."

"You're making a mistake, Hayes. You're really not seeing clearly here."

"Out!" I yell, and finally he leaves.

Mom brings me a mug of cold Swamp Brew an

hour later. I try to explain about the deposit and apologize again, but she just cuts me off.

"Stop embarrassing yourself, Hayes," she says as she sets down the tea. "Because you're starting to embarrass me too."

She leaves and I gulp the cold brew gratefully, hoping it'll put me right to sleep. But this time, the tonic doesn't work. I still feel panic racing through me. My stomach is still unsettled. My skin itches. My mind whirls, and my thoughts drift back to Owen Bailey.

One thing the Buzzards never talk about is death. They'll talk about roots, and how they think the world works, and how to manipulate those workings for one's own ends, but they aren't very forthcoming about the afterlife.

I feel restless. I want to go outside, get out of this house that's closing in on me. I can hear my mom downstairs on the phone, and I know she's talking about me. I go to my window. I've never even thought about sneaking out before, but maybe it's easy. I look out, and there, in Pulaski Square, I see something that makes me freeze.

It's the man. The one from the road. He's standing there, half hidden in the shadows, but his face is turned up to my window, and the light catches it. The sun is setting, and there's barely enough light to see him by, but I can still make out that he's dressed all in gray... and that his eyes are stitched shut.

16

Magnolia League Executive Meeting, Number 442
Senior Four only
Miss Lee presiding
Refreshments: Mrs. Pettit

"As the first order of business," Sybil McPhillips announces, "I move that we replace Dorothy Lee as the president of the Magnolia League, effective immediately."

The other members of the Senior Four all look up from their day planners and stare at her as though a dancing Chihuahua just leaped up onto her head. And then they look over to Dorothy herself, who appears strangely impassive.

"I second the motion," Mary Oglethorpe pipes up after an obligatory moment's consideration.

"This is neither the time, nor the place—" Khaki Pettit begins.

"It *is* the time, and most certainly the place," Sybil insists. "We have a second; I move for a vote."

Everyone looks at Dorothy to gauge her reaction, but she simply... yawns.

"Excuse me," she says, covering her mouth.

"Do try to stay awake, Dorothy!" Sybil snaps. "We are talking about removing you from your position."

"So I gather."

But the truth is, Dorothy Lee is exhausted. She may look like she's thirty-seven, but she feels like she's a hundred years old, ever since Jonathan Bailey started calling her at all hours of the night, crying. Naturally, she hates the sound of a crying man, but it would take a coldness even she doesn't have to hang up on him.

"Why'd the birds peck out his eyes?" Johnny sobbed into the receiver last night. "I just don't understand. All I wanted was to bury all my boy's parts together. Why couldn't I have that? Dorothy?"

Dorothy knows exactly why. The Gray Man wants

to see. She should know better than anyone. Some spirits—duppies, hags—run away the second you say *boo*, but Dorothy has spent all her life steering clear of spirits like the Gray Man and the Rondolier boy. Simple fools might tamper with them, but if you were wise, you didn't want any proof of that. Because those spirits have sick appetites. Between Johnny Bailey calling her at all hours, and the thought that the Gray Man was walking the streets of Savannah, sleep didn't come easily to Dorothy Lee.

And so it goes, day after day. Not to mention that Hayes Anderson spotted the beast herself. Thank goodness she had the sense to hide in the old church. Dorothy never would have guessed Hayes was as clever as all that. Of course, there was no way Dorothy was going to acknowledge the danger, not in front of these socialites thirsty for her title. The only reason she knows is because she glimpsed the murderer's work before, many years ago.

"Mother always said trouble is just opportunity in work clothes," Sybil continues. "Things have taken a turn, but I think it has given us an opportunity to take out the trash. I'm afraid, Dorothy, you have become the trash."

"Have your vote, then," Dorothy snaps, sick of the posturing. "No one's stopping you but your own flapping jaw."

"First, I would like to say that this is not some

caprice. You are detrimental to the League. You have allowed us to become embroiled in this fund-raiser that is falling apart at the seams. And, what is most serious, you have violated The Three."

This accusation takes Dorothy by surprise.

"Really. Pray tell me what you mean."

"You have tampered with the dead."

"How?"

"You *know* how."

"I'm afraid you'll have to explain it to me, sister."

"I've heard it from an unimpeachable source," Sybil McPhillips says. "My daughter. She says that Doc Buzzard told her that you were breaking The Three and thus we have to deal with you or *he* will."

Dorothy suddenly stands and pulls her car keys out of her purse.

"Let's go, sisters. Let's drive on out to the Roost, the four of us, and ask Doc about that. Let's hear it from his own lips. Not to cast aspersions on your darling daughter, Sybil, but she does sometimes get confused between what people tell her and what the pinot grigio might have to say."

Sybil opens and closes her mouth, trying to think of a comeback, but for the moment she's at a loss. Dorothy presses her advantage.

"In fact, let's go take a Clear Sight ritual with Doc, the four of us together, because I've been wondering about some things myself. Like, what we're doing about Jonathan Bailey's son?"

"Why should that be *our* responsibility?" Sybil manages.

"Because his boy was taken by the Gray Man, and I happen to think you raised him up, now that we're on the topic of The Three."

"Don't you try to distract everyone with wild accusations," Sybil says, forcing herself to give a laugh that comes out harder than necessary, and insufficiently sincere. "You think some teenager out of his head on beer is my fault? I am not some killer of children, Dorothy, and if you think so, then you've taken leave of your senses."

"I've got half a mind to slap you upside your head, sister," Dorothy says. "The smart people around here have a hard time believing in natural death when that passing has every hallmark of the Gray Man, and if you still doubt me, then check your charms. I wake up every morning and find the haint liquor on my back porch drunk up and the salt on my doorstep turned black, like someone's been trying to step over it. Who's that if it's not the Gray Man? He took the poor boy's eyes. What more do you want? His calling card?"

"I just don't see why it's suddenly *our* fault," Sybil says. "Who's to say a Magnolia did it, sister?"

"If he's out there, someone obviously called him

up. So, well, who? Was it you, Sybil? Or was it Mary? Was it Khaki? I certainly hope it was one of you, because if it was the Buzzards, then something has changed in our relations with them, and they're lying to us with their faces and working mischief with their hands, and I don't find *that* a very comforting thought."

There's silence for a moment as all of this sinks in. Dorothy's mind turns to Louisa somehow losing the buzzard's rock and crashing her van the next day. She wonders about Alex almost dying in a car accident, just like her mother. How far can the Gray Man travel? Could he make it all the way to California?

"Sam and Doc would never do that," Sybil says. "See, this is exactly the kind of rumormongering and paranoia that makes you unfit for your duties as president of the League, Dorothy. The Buzzards are our friends, and I trust our friends to protect us."

"Maybe you trust them a bit *too* much," Dorothy responds. "Our charms and protections are only as good as what the Buzzards taught us, and we all know Doc has only ever been in this for himself. If the Gray Man is loose, someone powerful brought him here, and I don't see any other candidates."

"Why you're carrying on this way I simply don't know," Sybil says. "But I believe we all were about to hold a vote."

"Then hold your silly vote," Dorothy practically spits. "Just stop yapping about it."

"I believe you'll be required to leave the room," Sybil says. "This should be a secret ballot."

"Oh, Lord, take me now." Dorothy sighs. "I am not going anywhere. Up or down, ladies. Let's get this farce over with."

"I'm sorry. I just don't think it's proper that you be here."

"Sybil, honestly — we can hold an oral vote," Mary says. "All in favor of asking Dorothy Lee to step down as president of the Magnolia League, say 'aye.'"

There's a loud "aye" from Sybil. Khaki sits like she's made of stone. After a moment, Mary gives a quiet "nay."

"We've been best friends since St. James Nursery," she says apologetically to Sybil.

"So we're split," Dorothy snaps. "Sorry, Sybil, but you should know better than to let your mouth write checks your fanny can't cash. Now that we're through with all this carrying on, I believe we need to address the fact that the Gray Man is among us."

"True, but there are more pressing matters, darling," Sybil says, recovering her poise appallingly quickly. "This fund-raiser. We have no caterer."

"That's because your granddaughter forgot to pay him."

"Oh, I've had enough of you, Dorothy Lee," Sybil sputters. "You've got all the manners of a chigger-bit *porch* hound."

"Both of you, cut it out!" Khaki Pettit barks. "You two are supposed to be setting an example. Not for your children—it's far too late for them. Louisa's dead, and Ellie favors her liquor a bit too much, if you don't mind my saying. But your public brawling is making its mark on your *grand*children now. You're setting them at each other's throats, teaching them to grow up to be hateful old women. So for their sakes, at least, you two need to stop this foolishness once and for all."

There is an embarrassed silence.

"I am fed up with the rudeness in here," Sybil says, pushing back. "I'll join you three later when the air is a little less thick with self-righteousness."

And with that she huffs out of the room.

"Khaki's right," Mary says, now that it's just the three of them. "If you keep on feuding this way with Sybil, Alex and Hayes are going to grow up the same way."

"If they haven't already," Dorothy says grimly.

Alex

According to Sina's directions, to get to Coachwhip Island, you have to drive out to Wassaw. But before you get to the turnoff, she explained, look for the signs for Coachwhip Island. Sometimes they're there, and sometimes they're not. If you see a sign, take the turn right away.

There're only two roads on Coachwhip. People call them This Road and That Road. Park your car and ask around, she said. Someone may know where

Dr. Jacobs is. Or not. He might actually be dead by now. But even so, someone should know how to find him.

"So let me understand," I said to Sina before setting off on this journey. "I go out looking for signs that may or may not be there, to find a man who may or may not be dead, so that he can tell me how to get my mother back? Sorry if I'm finding this all a little vague."

"Mmmm-hmm. Well, that's the space in between life and death. Not going to find *that* on your GPS, are you?"

So here I am, keeping my eyes peeled for signs to Coachwhip Island, while beside me my phone buzzes away like an angry hornet.

"Hello?" I shout over the noise of the Mini. "Can't the musicians just play as a trio? Hold on, it's my other line.... Hello? Mrs. McPhillips said what? I'm sorry but, no, *my* grandmother would absolutely *die* if there were any Gerbers in the centerpieces.... I'm just trying to save you time. Hold on, that's my other line...."

Dude. I used to think that party planners were idiots. But nope—in fact, they're geniuses. They've gotta be. Food has to be timed, along with the music, musicians' breaks, and, *hello*, will anyone present be allergic to peanuts? And I thought we had world peace to figure out. Peanuts!

The table rental place is now telling me it will only take cash. Oh God—can there possibly be another problem? At exactly that moment, I see a piece of plywood, propped up against a palmetto, that has the word *Coachwhip* spray-painted across it and an arrow pointing down a road that I'm about to pass at full speed. I take the turn so fast my tires squeal, but I just make it, slowing down as I drive along the narrow road with nothing but marsh on either side.

Thankfully, the phone cuts out as I leave the broken-up asphalt and hit the island itself. I slow down and look around me. I'm not sure if I'm on This Road or That Road, but it's yellow sand and extends straight ahead through a tunnel of live oaks and cabbage palmettos. Spanish moss hangs from their branches, and resurrection ferns grow all the way up their trunks, making them look as if they're covered with some sort of green fur, while all around their massive bases are shorter, scruffier saw palmettos and stunted red-bay trees. The sand of the road is thick now, so I figure I should park and walk. The last thing I want is to get my tires stuck out here in the late afternoon, with no phone service.

I stop the car and get out. It's weirdly hot for late winter, and before I've gone out of sight of the Mini, my throat is dry. Dappled sunlight burns right through the live-oak canopy and scorches my skin. In the trees I can hear the raspy smoker's chirp of marsh wrens and the occasional *pirp pirp pirp* of a piping plover. A transparent ghost crab scuttles across the sandy road in front of me before vanishing into the underbrush.

I walk for about twenty minutes but still don't see anyone who can tell me where Dr. Jacobs's office might be, and I'm beginning to doubt that there's so much as a shack, let alone a doctor's office, on Coachwhip. Then I hear the soft clopping of what sounds like coconut shells behind me, and I turn to see an old black man plodding up the road on the back of a scruffy, tired-looking horse. The horse is swaybacked, and it's clearly just looking for a place to lie down and die. The man doesn't look much better. His face is shiny and greasy and looks as if it's been folded and refolded a dozen times. He's wearing shorts and a stained navy-blue blazer. Improbably, he's also wearing a busted old top hat, and in one hand he holds a bent umbrella that looks like he pulled it out of the trash.

"Afternoon." He nods as he passes me.

"Afternoon. Um—excuse me?"

He turns, but his horse keeps putting down one slow foot after another.

"Yuh?"

"Do you know where Dr. Jacobs's office is?" I feel like an idiot. Clearly this guy has never even seen the inside of a doctor's office. But to my surprise, he takes my question in stride.

"Come on up this way, and I'll take you to the doctor," he says.

And so I trot along next to his horse. It's not hard to keep up. The horse gives me a resentful look, then proceeds to ignore me.

"So do you actually know Dr. Jacobs?"

"Much as any fellow know himself," he says. " 'Cause Dr. Jacobs is me."

"Wait—you're a doctor? You?"

Without looking at me, the man reaches into his sport coat and pulls out a dirty piece of paper and hands it to me. I unfold it. It's an old Columbia Medical School diploma granted to Dr. Jacob Jacobs. The paper is softened and worn away at the edges and folds.

"Oh—well. It's nice to meet you."

"Not sure yet."

"What?"

"Not sure yet if it's nice to meet *you*."

"Oh. Um, okay. Well, do you want to know what I want? Or should we go to your office?"

"One place is as good as the next," he says. "As for what you want, I doubt you even know what you want. That's why you've come t'see Dr. Jacobs, isn't it?"

"No, I know what I want. I want my—"

He reins his horse, and it grudgingly comes to a stop.

"You know what the coachwhip snake is?" he asks, cutting me off.

"Is that what they named this island after?"

"It's a legendary viper, full of poison and hate. It senses breath, and after it strikes, it sticks its head right up to your nose holes t'see if you're still breathing. If you are, it wraps itself around your face and strikes at you again and again until you *are* dead. That's the coachwhip snake. You know why I'm telling you that?"

"No."

At this point, I'm beginning to seriously doubt that Dr. Jacobs graduated from Columbia Medical School.

"'Cause you're about to step on one."

I look down, and two feet in front of me is a three-foot-long snake, as thick and black as an inner tube, basking in the sun. I freeze, and then it spins around in a circular motion before weaving its way into the underbrush, leaving me shaking.

"Girl don't got the sense not to step on a coachwhip. How can she know what she wants?"

"I didn't see it."

"Why weren't you looking? Bound to be a few lying about here and there if we named the damned island after 'em."

All right. Obviously, there's not a lot to be gained by arguing with this Yoda.

"Okay—so how do I figure out what I want?"

"*That*'s why you've come to Dr. Jacobs," he says, as if I'm the slowest student in class. "You trust me now. I am a doctor."

And then...he falls off his horse.

Maybe this is how he gets down, but he's so old that he just sort of slumps and slides off to one side and then hits the sand bonelessly. I yelp and rush to pick him up, but he's already clambering to his feet, joints popping and cracking like soft little rifle shots. His horse doesn't even turn to look, just swishes its tail to keep off the deerflies.

"Are you all right?"

"Everyone comes to Dr. Jacobs for two things," he says with the voice of the weariest of tour guides. "To learn what they want and to learn how to *get* it. I always tell them the truth. 'Course, sometimes I give the right thing to the wrong person and they wind up dying. See, my medicine don't work for everyone. Some of them are allergic."

"Oh. Well, can you tell if it'll work for *me*?"

"Not till you try it. Now quit squirming, and let me make my diagnosis."

I gotta say, this dude smells the way the field crew did back at the RC after they spent the day working the fields in the summer—sharp, oniony, and greasy. But Sina sent me here for a reason, so I try to breathe shallow while Dr. Jacobs grabs my face and holds it between his two leathery hands.

"Mmm," he says before turning my head to the right and left. "Mmm-hmmm. Mmm-mmm-mmm."

He shakes his head sadly.

"What?"

"You got a fat face."

"I do *not.*"

"You trying to hide it underneath all these hexes and roots you've pulled down over it, but my diagnosing hands don't lie. You got yourself a fat little face."

I try to wriggle away. I've kinda gotten used to all of these Magnolia charms, and the idea that he sees through them is unsettling.

"Got them Buzzards snappin' at you," he says. "Workin' you, pullin' you around, moving you from here to there all over the place."

And then he falls silent again, his eyes rolled up to the canopy of live oaks and Spanish moss overhead. His gaze darts from side to side, as if he's reading a book that's stuck in the branches up there.

"Mmm," he says. "Mmm-hmm."

"Are you just going to stand there humming, or are you going to tell me what to do?"

"Little girls with fat faces oughtta respect their elders," he says, taking his hands away. "You just want to be a little baby again, don'tcha? You don't want to grow up. You were mindin' your own business, and then one day death come creeping in your room, steal your mama away? That's how it went, huh?"

"My mom died."

"That's right," he says. "I know your mama. I know where she is too. And now you want her back.

You're selfish, though. You're going to hurt everyone round you 'cause you want your mama."

My cheeks burn with embarrassment. He's right— I mean, looking at it this way, what I'm doing is ugly and wrong. I think about Hayes and how I set her up to be humiliated in front of her grandmother. I think about Owen Bailey and how scared he must have been when the Gray Man came to meet him. I think about Thaddeus trying so hard to save me from something and how I've pushed him away. Why am I ruining everyone who tries to help me? When I got here, all I wanted was my old, simple life in the hills of California. But what I'm after has gotten much, much more complicated than that, and I've gotten more complicated too.

"You know, I didn't come out to the middle of nowhere just to get the same insults I can get from Sina back at the Roost."

"Then why'd you come out here?" Dr. Jacobs says.

"This is going nowhere. Forget it," I say over my shoulder as I walk away. And he lets me. Doubling back the way I came, I see that the greenery has grown even thicker, the vines wrapped into thick knots.

And then he calls out to me: "If you want to help your mama, you got to hold a funeral."

I shake my head, exasperated. "We had one, Dr. Jacobs. Almost a year ago."

"Midnight funeral," he says. I turn around to face

him. But he just stands there, so I give in and walk back. "The only time you can catch spirits going from one day to the next," he continues. "That's the only way you're going to get what you want."

"Can you be more specific? Do I go get her body or something?"

"Midnight funeral, I said. What else you need to know, Fat-Face?"

"You know what? Fine." My voice is shaking with anger. "Thanks for no help at all."

But as I make my way toward the car, one more thought stops me.

"Dr. Jacobs," I yell. "You know the Gray Man?"

"'Course I know the Gray Man." He smiles, his yellow teeth glistening. "Will Long and I are old friends."

I rub the buzzard's rock in my pocket, then take a deep breath. "Well, I need to kill him."

The doctor tips his head back and laughs. "He's already dead," he says, finally containing himself.

"I need to make him more dead."

He narrows his eyes at me. "What for?"

"He tried to kill me. And now he's after—"

"You're the one?" Dr. Jacobs raises his eyebrows. "All that trouble for a little fat-face like you?"

"What trouble?" I say fiercely. "Do you know something about this?"

The doctor shakes his head. "Can't say, can't say.

Won't tell anyone about your funeral, can't tell you about a conjurer. But you're not gonna get rid of William Long. Not unless you die yourself. And even then—I don't see much chance for a little waddler like you against a thing like that."

By now I've had it. This isn't just about my mom anymore. This is about my friends.

"You've put kids in danger!" I yell. "You've killed someone by bringing up this...thing! You tell me how to put him back under. *Now*."

The doctor practically spits his words at me. "You little priss. I told you. I can't undo what I done for another conjurer. That's against our laws. I told you what to do for your mama. I told you where William Long comes from. Man likes whiskey. Man likes raw meat. Use your noggin' to learn the rest." He spits on the ground, then turns and goes back to his horse.

I sprint back down the road to my car. When I look back, there's no trace of him—no horse, no man. It's as if I dreamed it. When I pull out, my tires kick up sand and I bump along the dirt road and then the broken asphalt until I'm back on the highway. The sign to Coachwhip Island is gone now, and I'm not surprised at all.

As soon as I get back into reception range, my phone starts buzzing again. The caterers are willing to hire extra staff, Mrs. McPhillips says. And they managed to find a fourth musician, so we'll have a string quartet after all. I try to act like I care, but *whatever*. Why do I have to pretend to care about these things when I'm trying to figure out how to keep people alive?

When I get back to the Roost, I spot Sam, who's just coming out of his garden across the compound. He waves, but I pretend not to see him and hurry into Sina's cottage instead.

"Hey," she says, looking up from her altar table, which is draped in blue cloth. "Find him?" she asks.

"Yeah, he was a real winner."

"What did he say?"

"That I have a fat face."

"Well, you did. He always could see through the charms."

"It was a total washout. We're back to square one."

"No, Dr. Jacobs is smart. If he saw you and saw through your charms, then he also must have seen what you wanted and told you how to get it. Think hard."

I shake my head. "He said that the only thing for my mom was to give her a funeral. A midnight funeral, he said."

"He said that?"

"Yeah. Something about when the spirits go—"

"From one day to the other." Sina stares at me. She looks serious. "I was afraid of that."

"What?"

"Look, I promised I'd help you," she says. "Like I said, we have a deal. But—I don't know if this is right."

"If *what's* right?"

"Midnight funeral is deep hoodoo. Practically voodoo. Different gods. Dark stuff."

"Oh." My chest starts to thump. I have to do something even scarier than the exorcism? Am I up for this?

"All right, well, if this is what we have to do, then we have to do it. We're way too far along to quit now. You promised me."

"I did. And I'm not going to back out, either, but you should know...this could cause a lot of harm. Not just to you but to everyone you know. We do something like this, we're down deep in the hole. It's petro magic, understand?"

"Sure," I say, though I have no idea what she's talking about.

"If we do it, there's no turning back. You need to understand that."

"Sina," I say as clearly as I can, exasperation getting the better of me. "I've alienated myself from my friends. My grades are tanking. And I've broken up with the only guy who's ever loved me. Why in hell would I turn back now?"

My phone buzzes again. It's the florist. Won't these people leave me alone?

"There's something else Dr. Jacobs and I talked about, Sina," I say quickly. "The Gray Man. Getting rid of him. How to send him back under."

Sina shakes her head. "You're not strong enough for that, girl. Put that out of your head, now."

"I can't, Sina. He's loose. He's killing people. Owen Bailey, for one. Not the greatest guy I ever met, but he didn't deserve to die."

Sina nods reluctantly.

"I think Hayes might be next."

Sina stands and goes to the window, playing absent-mindedly with the curtain.

"Listen," she says. "You're not my favorite person, though till now I've admired your gumption. But the Gray Man—you can't fight him. He's worse than the devil himself. If you take on the Gray Man, you'll lose."

"Dr. Jacobs said maybe if I went to the In Between—"

"No, I'm sorry. I'll try to protect your friends, but you need to focus on one thing at a time. Who do you care about more, your mama or these new people who barely know you?"

"That's not a fair question."

"Listen," she says, turning to me. "We can get to Louisa. We can *get* to her. This other thing is a distraction, and we can't do both. So let's focus on this funeral." She sighs heavily. " 'Cause you'll be lucky if you survive that part at all."

18

Hayes

No one loves a party more than I do. After all, social-izing is an art. I carefully choose which functions to attend, what to wear, what time to arrive, whom to talk to, how long to talk to them, when I should leave. Even the most odious, boring gathering can deliver a real satisfaction to me. The preparations above all. But in the case of the Louisa Lee Memorial Greenhouse Gala, I honestly just can't find it in me. I have abso-lutely no desire to go.

"Why aren't you ready?" my mother barks from the door to my room. "My God, what do you have on? Navy blue at an outdoor event? The last time I checked, you were over eight years old. Where is your mind, Hayesie?"

How can I explain? Navy blue (with scarlet piping) is precisely how I feel. The last place on earth I want to be is where the only thing people are talking about is Alex—how wonderful she is. How she put together such an *amazing* gathering. How she pulled it off at the last *minute*. How I fell down on the job and she had to push me aside and pick up the pieces because I just wasn't capable.

"Do I *have* to go?"

"Do you have to go?" My mother looks at me like I have the world's largest pimple on the end of my nose. "Lord God, don't talk nonsense."

"Tell them I'm sick," I plead. "Tell them I've got something contagious. Tell them I've been abducted. Just don't make me go to this thing."

"Look, I know you're embarrassed about shirking your duties," my mother says, safe behind her third Chardonnay of the day. "But you need to take it like a woman. Your grandmother wants both of us there, and I'd suggest you don't disappoint her any further, hmm?"

So I trade the navy dowager frock that actually expressed how I feel for a more festive color-blocked

Milly maxi dress. Still, something's not right. Normally when I get ready to go out, I sparkle. Right now I've got about as much glow as a mug of pond water. If I had a single charm with any power left, I'd try to do something about my appearance, but I never had time to go to Sam or Sina to renew a thing. Out of desperation, I went to the drugstore today and picked up a cartload of products that women with no magic at their disposal use. Tonight I spent two hours with a pair of tweezers to get my face looking right, and I've had to cover up my rapidly devolving skin with a truckload of foundation and cover-up. By the end, I look only okay, and I'm exhausted. I can't believe the other girls out there go through this.

My mother and I don't talk in her car on the way over. It's not far, but we're both wearing heels so high it's impossible to walk. When we arrive, I note the glass hasn't been put into the greenhouse yet. But whereas three days ago it was just a giant white frame, now a veritable jungle of plants drapes the entire building. As with anything planned by the Magnolias, the party is absolutely gorgeous; it looks like the walls and roof are made of flowers and vines—pink azaleas, drooping purple wisteria, yellow jasmine. Caterers in white shirts and black pants dash all over the lot carrying tables, cables, cases of white wine, silver chafing dishes of food. Underneath the curtain of flowering plants, every beam and board has been wrapped in white fairy lights. Eighteen tables fill the room, with one end still left open for dancing. At the center of each table is a huge, clear glass bowl filled with water, and in the middle of each bowl floats a single, spotless cream-colored magnolia.

The string quartet is tuning up in the corner, the air is scented with flowers, and I'm just starting to feel like I'm coming out of my funk, when my grand-mother digs her talons into my arm.

"You're here," she says, pulling me toward the front of the greenhouse. "Good. You have one job tonight, Hayes, all right? Try not to mess it up."

"Please don't treat me like that."

"Like what?"

"Like I'm stupid. I'm your granddaughter. I know you haven't been happy with me, but I just keep trying to get it right and—"

"You are *not* going to cry and ruin your makeup," my grandmother snaps. "I absolutely forbid it. I will treat you according to your behavior. And right now that means I must treat you like a small child who does not know how to comport herself, who loses checks, who can't pay people on time, and who doesn't pull her own increasing weight." She looks me up and down. "Did you check in with Sam about your Canar-ies and your spells? Because right now...let's just say the bloom is off the rose."

I look around to make sure no one's hearing this.

196

"Please . . ."

"Now—you'll be working coat check. People give *you* their coats, *you* give them a *ticket*. Try to manage it, will you?"

So here I am, one hour later, hustling coat hangers while Savannah's best and brightest walk into the party of the season. The old-money Buchanans, the medically accomplished Joyner-Chandlers, the incredibly philanthropic Rampersants, the criminally good-looking Vanderhorsts. Men are in black tie, women are in gowns, and everyone was warned to wear tennis shoes because of the soft dirt floor (though, of course, no one actually has).

"Thank you so much for doing this," Alex whispers, coming back from her post as greeter. She looks fantastic in a close-fitting, ankle-length silver-white satin dress. Lord, we conjured this girl *way* too well. My brother will absolutely die. She kisses me on both cheeks, the way my grandmother used to do. I know now, of course, that the more someone kisses you, the less you can trust that person. Alex smells of ginger and sassafras, which means she's been drinking Watch Over Me tea, and her hands are clammy, as if she's nervous.

I try a joke. "White dress?" I say lamely. "You getting married, or up to a ritual or something?"

Alex gives me a look I can't read, but she definitely doesn't laugh.

"Sorry. I'm trying to break the ice here, Alex."

She shakes her head and is about to say something, when her grandmother swoops in. "Come along, Alex."

I watch her walk into the rapidly expanding crowd. Everyone she passes gives her a party-sincere look, condolences, an earnest grip of the hand, or a kiss on the cheek. I start to feel ill.

"Hey."

Just when I thought it couldn't get any worse: Jason. He's with his parents, and standing next to him is Anna. I don't understand. I knew his parents were invited, but what is this? I can't manage to get my mouth to move.

"Hello, Hayes," his mother says coolly.

"Mrs. Emory," I manage. "You look lovely tonight."

"And so do you. I'm sorry to weigh you down with these...." She hands over two heavy coats.

"Don't worry about it," I say automatically. "I'm just doing my part."

I give them their tags, and his parents move off, but Jason stays because Anna wants to give me her wrap.

"It's *so* warm in here," she says.

"I bought two tickets to support Alex," Jason says. "Figured you'd be working, so I thought you wouldn't mind if I brought Anna."

"Of course not."

Although, actually, I do mind. I mind more than I can possibly express.

"Isn't this amazing, you know, that Alex put this all together for her mom?" Anna says.

"Amazing," I repeat dully.

"Well, anyway," Jason says, sensing the awkwardness of the situation. "When the dancing starts, maybe I'll come get you. We can do the funky chicken, right? Or whatever it is all these old people do."

They move off, and I realize that while his hand is on Anna's arm, he didn't touch me once. No hug, no kiss, not so much as a peck on the cheek. Though I know it's as unwise to chase men as it is to run after buses, I hurry across the room nonetheless.

"Um, can I talk to you for a second?"

"Sure," Jason says, looking uncomfortable.

I pull him over to a pillar wrapped in fairy lights and wisteria.

"Uh, are we broken up?"

"What?"

"Are we broken up?"

He's looking right into my eyes. God, he's good-looking. I mean, if I had just kept the charms up... How did I get so lazy? My grandmother's right: I am stupid.

"Yes," he says finally. "I guess. I mean, Hayes—you've been so into your own problems and the Magnolia stuff lately, I don't even think you care if I'm around or not. I just got tired of it, I guess."

"Oh." Well, he doesn't have to make it any clearer.

The sudden loss of his affections. The incredible speed with which he's gotten tired of me. The charms I put on him were fading, but not like this. His change of heart wouldn't be this severe if it were due to natural causes. Obviously, Alex has put a Crush Killer on him.

"Well, I guess I don't have anything to add to that."

"Okay," he says. "I'm sorry it worked out this way."

"Me too."

He pats my arm. "I feel bad this went on for so long," he says. "We should have talked about all this a while ago. I don't even remember the last time we had fun together."

Of course he doesn't. He's been rooted. But it won't be this way for long. I'm a Magnolia. I've got charms Jason will never understand—literally.

Spinning on my heel, I march back to the coat check. Suddenly, I'm filled with something completely unfamiliar—rage. Real, coursing, visceral rage. Alex has ruined everything for me. My social standing. My relationship. My claim to the leadership of the Magnolia League. My grandmother has been right all along. I need to take Alex down.

Cold beads of sweat start to form on my forehead. I could go to Sina for a charm against Alex. But this is more serious. I want more. It's a completely strange sensation, cold and hot and seductively evil. There's no question what the answer is here, and it's like nothing the old me ever would have dared to think.

I want to Blue Root the bitch.

"Hey," Madison says, appearing out of the crowd. "It's just her nature."

Madison and Dexter. How wonderful. More people to see me working here like the hired help.

"You're right," I growl. "Alex ruins everything."

"Not Alex," Madison says. "Anna. It's in her nature to go after what you've left behind."

"Since when did I leave Jason behind?"

"Someone's left *somebody* behind," Dexter says, with something less than tact. "Because he's all over Anna like spray tan."

Madison jabs him with her elbow. She looks great. Being in love suits her. Her pale skin looks smooth and poreless, and that red Zac Posen dress contrasts beautifully.

"I'm glad you're here, actually," I say. "I need you to help me take her down for good."

"Whoa," Dex says. "Anna's already kind of a lint-brain, Hayes. Is a takedown really necessary?"

"Not Anna," I say impatiently. *"Alex."*

"Dude," Dex says, "you sound like a bad action movie. You want to take Alex down? She's been acting weird, yeah. But she's our friend. And it's her mom's friggin' memorial."

"Okay, Dex," Madison says, stepping around the table and taking my arm. "What say you make up for your big mouth by manning the coat check for a bit?"

"What? Oh, crap."

"Now."

"I'm an idiot," he grumbles as Madison marches me out of the greenhouse.

Madison walks me into the police barracks across the street, where the gala guests have use of the bathrooms for the evening. She closes the door and I look in the mirror—I look even worse under these lights.

"What the hell is wrong with you?" she asks.

"It's Alex," I seethe. I know I probably should be hiding my rage, but I can't help it. "She made me look like an idiot. My grandmother thinks I can't do anything right, my mother thinks whatever my grandmother thinks, and it's all Alex's fault. Plus, I'm positive she Crush Killed Jason."

Madison shakes her head, exasperated. "Hazer, no one is ruining your life. Seriously. You've hit the debutante dark place."

"Alex *rooted* me," I cry, spilling out my worst fears. "She's put the *bite* on me!"

"You need to get hold of yourself," Madison says. "This is not Alex's fault."

"Don't you start sticking up for her too!"

"I'm not sticking up for anyone."

"Look, unless you want to ruin our friendship..."

"Ruin?"

"Then stay out of my way. Because I'm going to

root her, Madison. I've got a lot of cash in my emergency fund. I can go to Doc Buzzard and pay him to get rid of her."

"All right." Madison sighs. "That's it."

"What?"

"You are officially out of control." She takes a deep breath. "So I need to tell you a couple of things."

"Stop defending Alex!"

"Hazer, shut *up* for a minute."

Madison's never told me to shut up before. It's enough to, well, make me speechless.

"Okay, first, my grandmother bought you something. But you need to get a grip before I show it to you. And you can't tell anyone about it, because if you do, we're all going to go down."

"That's really sweet of her, but I don't have time right now, I have to —"

"You'll want to see this. It's about Alex."

"What is it?"

"Promise you won't tell anyone."

"I promise I won't tell anyone. *God*, what's all the secrecy?"

"Okay," Madison says. "Come with me." She pulls me outside to the parking lot. "Get in," she says, opening the door to her car.

"Where're we going?"

"Back to the future."

It sounds like something Dexter would say. This is

probably just some kind of joke on her part to make me forget why I'm angry.

"I don't have time for games, Madison. I really have to get back to the party."

"If you don't get in, I'm going to tell your grandmother I found a strange vial full of white powder in your purse. That'll pretty much wrap it up between you and her, don't you think?"

Now my jaw has dropped practically to the ground, but she just stares at me with scary intensity. Obviously, I have no choice but to get into the car.

"This had better not take long."

"Just chill, all right? And stop acting like your grandmother for, like, five minutes. Okay. We need to find some water."

She drives a few blocks, taking the corners like a crazy woman. "This'll do." She jerks the wheel to the left, and we land squarely in the middle of the sidewalk in front of Columbia Square.

"Out," she commands.

She bursts out of the car, carrying her purse. Reluctantly I follow. The streetlights around the fountain are burned out—no big surprise in Savannah. This city is full of the dead, everyone knows that. The air is so thick with spirits, you can feel them all around you the minute you cross Abercorn into the old part of town. Dead souls, be they kind or mischievous, don't like streetlights, which is why half of them around here are always out. In fact, you can usually tell if a spirit's following you if the streetlights around you flicker or go out altogether.

Sitting on the lip of the fountain, Madison rummages through her purse and pulls out a green silk sack.

"What, are we going to make a wish or something?"

"Zip it."

Her brow wrinkles in concentration as she produces a glass vial and measures out exactly six drops of yellow liquid into the fountain. The water does seem to get a little thicker, but I'm not impressed. I let out a big sigh for her benefit.

"So you brought me out here to show me all the root work you've been practicing?"

"You know, I'm going to beat you like a redheaded stepchild if you don't hush up," she says, not looking up.

Now she takes out a handful of red clay and some white pepper and drops them into the fountain. Then, taking two birch sticks, she rubs them together four times and tosses them in too. Finally, she scoops up a handful of fountain water and drinks it.

"Mads, eeeeew. That stuff is filthy!" I mean, people *spit* in these things. And worse. But she's just sitting there on the lip of the fountain, hands folded, eyes closed, as if she's just taken a sip of Evian and is thinking really hard about it. Then she dribbles the water into her cupped hand, reaches down and mixes a little dirt with it, and stirs it with her finger. Closing her hand into a fist, she whispers something into it and then opens her hand, and a tiny frog hops out.

"Oh. My. *God*."

I've *never* seen this kind of hoodoo before. Where did she *learn* this? Just then there's a *pop!* and a gentle tinkle of glass, and a streetlight on the other side of the square goes out. Madison lifts the frog in front of her face and speaks to it:

> *Master creature, small and free,*
> *Bring this vision back to me.*
> *Master creature, small and free,*
> *Bring this vision back to me.*

She carefully places the frog in the fountain, and it disappears into the water.

I feel like I need to say something. This whole routine is making me seriously uneasy.

"Come on, Madison. This is getting really freaky, even for you."

She doesn't answer. I hear another *pop!* and another streetlight goes dark. Nothing happens for a long time and I want to say something, but I hold my tongue. When a spell doesn't work, which is fairly often, actually, it's not exactly nice to rub it in. But Madison doesn't seem worried.

Then I see movement in the water, coming from the other side of the fountain. The piece of birch is floating toward us. As it gets closer, I see that it's being pushed by the frog. The little creature swims right over to us, pushing the stick like a trained dolphin or something.

"Twenty-five," Madison commands. At which the frog dives underwater, and suddenly the fountain catches fire. Blue flames like burning vodka race across the surface of the water. They're huge and rising, and all I can think is that we are going to get in *so* much trouble.

"Madison, let's go, okay?"

But she grabs my arm and drags me closer. I look around to make sure no police are running over, and then I look into the fountain and see something soft and bright just beneath the fiery surface.

"What is that?" I ask, stepping back.

"Hold on—I can't make it out yet," she says. "But whatever it is, it's twenty-five years from now."

"The future?" I whisper, fear slamming through my veins. "You're pulling a Future spell?"

"No, Grandma Khaki conjured this. I'm just carrying it out." She looks at me for a second. "Anyway, why are *you* so holier than thou right now? You were about to Blue Root Alex."

"I was just saying that," I whisper. "I think."

"Were you? Look."

I force myself to look back into the fountain. It hurts my eyes, but after a minute they adjust and I see myself.

I look good, actually, twenty-five years from now. Hey, wait. *I look exactly the same.* I seem to have conjured myself at my current age. I know this can't be a true vision, because I've always known that it's greedy and foolish to conjure yourself too young. I never planned on staying this age forever. That's just so...desperate.

"Looks like you OD'd on the Youth-Dew," Madison says.

"Where am I?"

"Not sure. But I think you're at the front gate of Bonaventure."

I shake my head. Why am I alone? I look thin— too thin. And my eyes have dark circles under them, like my mother's. In fact, I seem to have picked up her habits, because there I am, taking out a flask of something in the middle of the afternoon. The other me takes a large swallow, then starts walking down a path in the graveyard.

"I'm visiting someone."

My heart is pounding. Who could be dead? Jason? Grandmother?

It looks like summer. Perspiration is pouring down my face. I'm wearing a blue linen dress, the same cut that my mother likes to wear, but I haven't taken care of it properly. It's wrinkled and marked with sweat.

I continue to walk down the dirt path, my heels wobbling in the sand. And then I wander into one of the grandest parts of the cemetery. I know it, because this is where we buried Louisa Lee's urn last year. Only the oldest families get to rest in this section. Then, stopping by a midsize marker, the future me kneels and opens a rather ostentatious purse. I throw down some chocolate and pour the rest of the whiskey onto the grave.

"There," the other me hisses. "Now leave me, you demon. You've got everything, okay? I'm alone, no friends, no family. So just *leave me be*."

I bend over the fountain, squinting so hard at the image that my head aches. And finally I'm able to see the words on the tombstone:

ALEXANDRIA LEE

1995–2012

"Oh my God," Madison says.

I back away, the image still rippling. "Madison. *Madison*. She's going to die."

"We can change this, though," Madison says. "Grandma Khaki conjured it to show us. She knows what's been going on between you and Alex. And she doesn't want a repeat of your grandmom and Dorothy Lee."

"Is this . . . ?" My stomach flips over. "Did *I* kill her?"

"Sort of looks that way," Madison says. "Or else you helped."

"Oh my God. I had this all wrong."

"Yup."

"I thought we were at war with each other. . . ."

"No, genius. That's what someone wants us to think. But we've got to stick together. There's something serious we have to deal with."

"Oh my God."

"You haven't done anything yet, have you?"

"No, but I wanted to."

"Like mother, like daughter."

"What?"

"Okay, Hayes—this is going to be the hard part, all right?" she says. "You're just going to have to trust me."

"What are you going to do?"

"What're *we* going to do," she corrects me. "We're going to save Alex's life, but it's not going to be fun or easy. Not for you, anyway."

Madison reaches into the fountain, right into the blue flame, and the second her hand touches the water, the image of me kneeling in front of Alex's grave ripples away, and the blue flames snap off like someone flipped a switch.

"Okay, fine. I'll do whatever you say."

"Not this time, Hayes. You spend way too much of your life doing what everyone else says. This time you need to make a decision. Are you able to drop this crazy grudge you've got against Alex?"

I think for a minute. Can I?

"I want to, but it's like I'm physically..."

"Unable. Right. It's the Gray Man. He turns people into their worst selves and—"

I turn to her, incredulous. "You believe me? About seeing him?"

She looks away, ashamed. "I didn't, I admit. I thought you were losing it. But I have believed for the last couple of days."

"What does that mean?"

"It means we need to get back to the party, Hayesie. There are some people we need to set straight."

19

Alex

Well, I was right. The streets of Savannah are as quiet as dawn on New Year's Day. Everyone who's anyone is at the party, which means I've got the whole town to myself.

Leaving before my grandmother's speech was a calculated risk. On the one hand, she'll almost certainly notice sooner that I've gone. On the other, having her stranded up there in front of everyone will buy me some extra time, and I need the head start. With luck, I'll be far away, and she'll have to deal with all the social upheaval that my absence will cause, before she can start looking for me.

I almost felt like a traitor to my mom by sneaking away from her memorial, but: real mom versus greenhouse named after her? There's no contest.

So with one quick Forget Me charm to make sure no one noticed my absence right away, I was up from the table, out the flower-draped front door, across the parking area . . . and I was gone.

Sina gave me strict instructions about tonight. When I get to the mansion, the first thing I do is strip it of protection. I sweep all the salt off the front and back porches, making sure it's away from the doors so spirits can go in and, more important, out. I go to the corner of the garden where I've seen Josie burying the paper bags of lye that keep spirits off the property, and I dig the bags up and throw them into the trunk of my car, along with the glass bottle full of bent nails and old pennies that was under the steps to the porch.

Now that the house is spiritually wide open, I unlock the door and run upstairs. All I have to do is get the door to the Blue Room open. I don't have a key, but I didn't watch all those old episodes of *Law & Order* on the RC's rabbit-eared TV for nothing. I back up to give myself some room and then kick the doorknob as hard as I can.

Instantly, pain shoots up my leg; it feels like a

ten-ton truck just slammed into the bottom of my foot. Okay. This is going to be more difficult than I thought. I brace myself and try again. This time there's a promising splitting sound around the doorknob. Twice more and I'm rewarded with a giant *cr-r-rack!*

I'm almost afraid to look. But yes. My mom is there, sitting alone on the bed. She's as pale as before, maybe even paler, wearing an old calico sundress I remember. It was always one of my favorites, but now it's torn and dirty. She's staring right through me, talking to someone who isn't there.

"Constance?" she asks. "What happened? Are we early?"

I want to kiss her and hug her and tell her that I'm finally getting her out of here, but I don't have the time and, besides, I know it'll just confuse her more.

"You can go now, Mom," I whisper. "The door is open."

"Constance?"

"We'll call you," I say. "Listen for Sina. We'll tell you where to go."

I'm not sure why I'm not supposed to put her in the car with me, but Sina said spirits travel on their own. So, leaving all the doors open behind me, I sprint to the Mini. According to Sina's plan, I need to get back so we can call her as soon as possible; otherwise, there's a chance she'll wander out and get as lost as she was before. As soon as I'm on the road, I speed-dial Sina.

"How is everything?" she asks.

"I did what you told me. The house is broken open, the charms are gone, and she's just waiting for your call."

"Get out to Coachwhip fast as you can," Sina says. "You'll need to drive down That Road until you see my lights. Go quick. We don't have much time."

Hanging up and tossing the phone onto the floor, I step on the gas and speed recklessly toward where I saw the Coachwhip Island sign before. This time, though, the plywood sign jumps into my headlights way too early, pointing down an entirely different road that heads in the opposite direction from the one I took before. I slam on my brakes and sit on the dark road for a minute, engine ticking. Is this a joke? Did someone move the plywood to mess with me? Or do I just not remember the way as well as I thought I did? But I've trusted Sina this far, and she said to follow the sign, so after a moment I turn down this strange, new road.

There's marsh on either side of me, but I don't rec-ognize anything else. The asphalt is cracked, all right, but the shoulders of the road have more palmettos on them than the other road did, and I'm about to make a U-turn and go back, when suddenly my tires are whis-pering along the familiar sandy track of This Road.

Or is it That Road? I see a wide sand path dodge off through the dark tunnel of trees to my right, and I take it. Then, before I know it, I'm turning again, and now I'm pretty sure I'm on That Road. Or else I was on That Road and now I'm on This Road. Just when I'm beginning to panic, up ahead I see a light shining through the live-oak trunks. I park and start running.

The air is humid and oppressive out here, even though back at the party it was at least fifteen degrees cooler. Mosquitoes are buzzing frantically in the dark, and I can smell salt water and pluff mud. The wind shifts the heavy tops of the palmettos, and the ground is soft beneath my feet. Within moments, I've reached the clearing.

Four Coleman camping lanterns hang in the trees, casting too-bright pools of white light. There's a big hole, large enough for a coffin, dug in the middle, and on the pile of black dirt next to it sits Dr. Jacobs. Sina, spotting me in the dark, hurries over.

"Did you take away all the charms?" she asks.

"Yeah. What's he doing here?"

"Dr. Jacobs? He liked you and wants to help out."

"Evening, Fat-Face," he says cheerfully, doffing his busted top hat.

I shake my head. "No. I don't want him here."

"I need help. You knew that. You didn't think I could ask Doc, did you?"

"I don't trust him."

"You trust me?"

"To hold up your end of the bargain, yes."

"Then I vouch for him. Besides, he's been doing lots of work for you Magnolia types recently. If he's good enough for the Andersons, he's good enough for the Lees."

"What's he been doing?"

"We don't have time to talk about that. You need to get ready."

"What do I do?"

"You're already wearing white. That on purpose?"

"Yeah."

"Good thinking." She looks me over. "Though that's an awfully nice dress for this dirty work."

"It's wash-and-wear."

Sina throws her head back and laughs. Dr. Jacobs hops off the pile of dirt and stretches.

"You ready, Doctor?" Sina asks.

"Ready as I'll ever be."

"What's he going to do?"

"Call for help."

"You said it was just us out here."

"I meant just us alive folks," Sina says. "Didn't say anything about the dead."

Dr. Jacobs sings out in a surprisingly loud voice:

"All you backward-facing men," he sing-shouts. "All you duppies, all you plat-eyes, I'm calling you.

Your mothers and daughters are looking for you. Your fathers and your brothers are out searching the marshes for you. Your sisters and your sons. I'm calling you up, you lost duppies, you backward people, I'm ringing you up out of the dirt. Get the fiddler crabs off your face, get the worms out your hair, make sure you look right, 'cause you've got kin looking for you. Come on up, duppies, pull your ribs off those roots, make sure you don't leave no bones behind, make sure you don't forget no pieces, duppies, make sure you got all your teeth. Get that gravel out your eyeholes, plat-eyes, get that dirt out y'all's mouth. Come up, come up, come up, 'cause y'all got kin looking for you, they been searching for y'all all night."

The air in the clearing thickens, and suddenly the lanterns seem to give off less light than before. The shadows get black and soupy, and I could be imagining things, but I think it's getting harder to breathe. Dr. Jacobs's voice is coming to me down a long tunnel, echoing like he's in an underwater cave.

Everything feels out of sync, as if sounds aren't matching up with movements. I can't tell how much time passes while Dr. Jacobs repeats himself over and over again, calling up duppies—whatever those are.

And suddenly he falls silent. There's a long pause, and then I hear a sound off in the trees—a strangled, choking noise. Then I hear it again right behind me, and there's an answering noise, rising and falling, truly awful, from not too far off to my right.

"Sina?"

"Hush."

The sound is all around us now, and I recognize it. It's crying. All around us in the dark, people are crying, wailing, letting loose as if the person they loved most has died. It's getting closer, and then people are stepping out of the trees and into the light. Some are howling, some are sniffling, sobbing, moaning, choking, but they're all shaking with tears.

And then I see something that almost makes me run: Their faces are all on backward. They walk forward stiffly and hesitantly, the backs of their heads facing forward and crying tears out of their backward eyes.

I look at Sina. She's smiling. Dr. Jacobs welcomes them and pours out a long stream of liquor from a whiskey bottle.

"Get the girl ready," he says. "I'll get the duppies to make up her bed."

He hands Sina the whiskey bottle, and she hands it to me.

"Drink it down," she commands.

"I don't want any."

"It's whiskey and gunpowder, girl. It's not to get you drunk—it's to keep you safe."

I choke down the burning liquid. It feels like it's

boiling in my stomach. I cough, and whiskey spills down my chin. Sina takes the bottle back.

"The next part is going to be hard, Alex. You're going to have to be brave."

"Of course."

"Don't 'of course' me. Do you want your mother back bad enough to do anything?"

"You know I do."

"Then just remember why you're doing this. Keep remembering it's all for your mother."

A cold trickle of fear runs down the back of my neck.

"Why? What happens next?"

She doesn't answer. Instead, she takes me by my shoulder and turns me around. The duppies have put a simple pine coffin on the ground next to the hole, and they're standing around it in a ring, forming a corridor leading from me and Sina to the coffin and the grave. Dr. Jacobs looks at me expectantly.

"Your girl ready for her midnight burial?" he asks.

"I've brought my girl, and she's ready to lie down," Sina says.

She pushes me forward. My legs don't want to work, so she walks with me, pushing me along in front of her.

"Get your daughters in their coffins." Dr. Jacobs giggles. "Get them down under a warm blanket of dirt."

"Wait. You didn't tell me about this part. I don't want to be buried, Sina," I whisper, panicking.

"It's for your mother, Alex. You said you'd do anything."

The blank backs of the duppies' heads are facing me, and they're rustling with anticipation as I walk down the line. Sina keeps pushing me, and the whiskey and gunpowder is making my arms and legs feel heavy and warm. It's like I've got a sun in my stomach, warming me from the inside. The dress feels rough against my skin.

"Lie down," Sina commands, and she steadies my shoulder as I find myself standing in the coffin. I don't want to be here.

"Why?" I say, trying to stall for time.

"We don't have Louisa's body," she explains impatiently. "It'd be impossible to do this at all if we didn't have you. You're her blood. You can pass for her at midnight."

"Sina—"

"Keep thinking about your mother, Alex." She takes my hand and sits me down in the coffin. "Drink this." She holds a cracked teacup to my lips.

I consider getting out of here, just pushing her aside and running, but I've come this far, and now there's no turning back. I open my mouth and gulp down the liquid. It's bitter and thick. As soon as I swallow it, I feel my head start to spin.

"You're not going to let anything bad happen to me, are you?" I ask, suddenly scared.

"This is all part of the ritual," Sina says, stroking my hair. "I'm holding up my part of the bargain. And so will you."

"Don't let me die, okay?" I say as I see three of the duppies pick up the coffin lid. I try to stand up, but my arms and legs are numb and rubbery.

"I'd never let you die," Sina says. "That's not what I want. Do you trust me?"

"Yes," I say as enthusiastically as I can.

"Well, honey." She grins wickedly. "I told you to never trust anybody."

Then she pushes me back into the coffin, and the duppies lay the lid over it, and I hear banging as they *nail it shut.*

I start to scream. I've never screamed before in my life, but right now I'm filling up this coffin with my shrieking. I'm banging on the lid so hard my wrists feel like they're breaking. I'm kicking and pounding and stubbing my bare toes and bruising my knees and elbows on the lid. Outside I hear a huge surge of sound as the crying duppies get louder, and then they're singing hymns, beating on the coffin, slapping it like a drum, pounding a complicated rhythm on its surface. They beat me into submission until I can't scream anymore, and finally I stop kicking on the lid, and their drumming gets louder and louder and louder.

Then it stops.

The world tilts. It feels like I'm flying as a hundred hands lift my coffin up, and then I'm rocking from side to side as they lower me into the grave. The motion stops, all the sound stops, and it's still and quiet and dark. There's a small thud—something's landed on the lid of my coffin. And then something else. Soon the muffled noises are coming faster and faster, and I realize that it's dirt. They're burying me alive.

Finally, it's completely silent. I can't even hear the duppies crying. The lid of the coffin creaks ominously under the weight of all the dirt piled on top of it. I'm running out of air. It's so dark that I can't tell whether my eyes are open or closed. I press on the lid, but it doesn't even bend a tiny bit. I want to open my mouth and scream, but it's so hot in here, I can't hear myself breathing.

And then, out of nowhere: Thaddeus. His face, right in front of me. Our kiss a couple of weeks ago, the one on the stairs. The air is running out. I can't breathe anymore. Yet that moment is so clear, as if it's happening all over again, right now. But even then, I knew what that kiss was, didn't I? A moment so precious, I'd take it all the way to my grave.

20

Hayes

Now that we know we have to change Alex's fate, naturally I feel the need to be quick about it. Warn her. Do *something*. But Madison has a different idea. She insists that we go back to the party and talk to my mother, of all people.

"I trusted you with the frog thing, but now you've lost your head," I say. "We need to figure out why Alex is in danger. Maybe find Sina or something."

"Babe, I happen to know why she's in danger. It's

dressed in Chanel and drinking a fourth G and T right about now."

"What on earth do you mean?"

Madison ignores me as she drives back through Savannah like a maniac. She double-parks near the greenhouse and yanks me toward it. Then she pulls me through the curtain of plants and drags me exactly where I don't want to go: my mom's table.

"Hayesie!" my mother gushes as we approach. "Where have you been? We've just been sitting here waiting for Alexandria to make a fool of Dorothy in front of the crowd." She smiles triumphantly, giving me a mock toast with her glass and then knocking back a third of it.

"What do you mean?"

"Well, from what I've heard, Alex has been acting quite hateful lately. Something's wrong with her, and now she's run out and left her grandmother hanging." She squints at us with bloodshot eyes. "Sit down, you're both making me nervous."

Madison clears her throat and addresses my mother. "Dex saw you going out to that island a few weeks ago," Madison said. "I think it's called Coachwhip or something? He thought it was weird since, you know, it's not really on Google Maps or anything, so he took me out there to check it out. Anyway, I got sort of obsessed with it, and then we sort of accidentally on purpose followed you out there one night, and you were doing some pretty crazy stuff."

"When?" I ask, incredulous. "What are you talking about?"

"That night before the oyster roast at Secession, when you got so mad that I ditched you," she says, smiling.

"Just wait one second," my mom says. "You were spying on me?"

"Yeah. We were pretty good at it too. We heard pretty much everything you said. Funny thing is, you were talking like you were speaking to someone else, but no one was there. You had a lot to say."

"What *is* this?" I demand. "You're talking about islands that aren't there? And people no one can see?"

"Patience, young one," Madison says. "Your mom knows what I'm talking about. She spent a lot of time on that island obsessing over Alex with her invisible buddy."

"Hayes," my mother says, "whatever trouble Louisa's child is in, it has nothing to do with us."

"Really?" Madison says. "Nothing to do with you?"

"Madison," my mom says, "I think you've had quite enough champagne tonight."

"Ellie," Madison says, using my mother's first name, "why don't you tell everyone about your awesome abilities. As a root doctor, I mean. I just think everybody would be very impressed that it was you who opened the door to the Gray Man."

"The what?" Thaddeus says, appearing out of nowhere and dropping his lanky self down in one of the chairs.

"Where have you been all night?" I demand.

"Looking for Alex."

"For the right reasons, I hope," Madison says. "Hard to tell where everyone stands these days. Especially in your family."

"What do you—"

"You'll have to catch up later," Madison says. "So, who's your invisible friend, Ellie? The one you asked to conjure up the Gray Man for you. Because we all know you're not actually smart enough to do it on your own."

"Where is your mother?" my mom asks. "I won't stand for this kind of behavior from a child."

"Won't stand for what kind of behavior?" my grandmother asks, joining us at the table.

"I'm just asking a question," Madison continues, mock-innocently. "Why all those long trips to Coachwhip Island?"

"Coachwhip?" my grandmother asks, her face turning pale. "Where'd you hear that name, Madison?"

"From your daughter. She's practically building a second house out there."

"I have no idea what she is talking about," my mother protests even as my grandmother turns on her.

"And what about all the fever leaf you've been

hoarding?" Madison continues with a cool smile. "Because, you know, a bunch of Magnolias have been looking for it, and every single bush is picked clean. The only place anyone'd be able to find it is in your attic, Mrs. A."

"How do you know that?" my mother says softly.

"I'm not just a pretty face," Madison says. "I mean, you have to admit that, as difficult as she is, some of Alex's problems—like, you know, being pursued by a demonic entity who wants to tear out her eyes—might have something to do with you."

"Ellie?" my grandmother asks. "What is she talking about?"

"You should be proud, Mrs. McPhillips," Madison says. "Your daughter seems to have managed to call up the Gray Man and put him on Alex all by herself."

"Ellie," my grandmother says dangerously. "Right now I want you to look me in the eyes and tell me that this is not true."

"When did you decide to start believing the drivel of drunk teenagers over your own daughter?" my mother says.

"Ellie?"

"It's not true," my mom protests in the voice she uses when she lies.

"So you're not smart enough to do it on your own?" Madison says, goading her.

"Stop babbling, Madison. You're worse than your

mother, always sticking your nose in where it doesn't belong."

"Oh, never mind, then." Madison smiles. "I guess I just overestimated you."

"Ellie," my grandmother says sharply. "Is this true or not?"

"Fine! It's true!" my mom shouts. Mr. and Mrs. Reddie, sitting at the nearest table, turn and look at us. My mom pauses for a second to collect herself before continuing. "I didn't do it on my own. I had a friend help me."

"You can't have," my grandmother says. "I don't believe you."

"Blah, blah, blah," my mother says recklessly. "The little snot's right. You should be proud of me, Mother. I found the right books, got the right ingredients, found the right person to assist. It took a long time to do all the research, but you know what good grades I used to get."

"You put a root on Alex?" I ask. I need to hear her say it.

"Not just a root," Madison says. "The Gray Man. Look him up sometime; he's a real charmer. He crawls inside people and brings out their worst selves. Then he makes them try to kill themselves. You know, slashed wrists, suddenly steering their cars into oncoming traffic, that kind of thing."

The last one makes my stomach turn to ice.

"You could have killed your daughter," my grandmother manages.

"I did it *for* my daughter," my mom hisses. "That Lee girl parachutes in and snatches everything away from Hayes. Hayes may have to be stuck here until she dies, but she doesn't have to be second-rate. My daughter is not going to be the towel girl for some little hippie who happens to have fallen out of Dorothy Lee's runaway daughter's womb on a marijuana farm in California. I spent my entire life being compared with the amazing Louisa Lee and coming up short. She was always the star, and I was always the consolation prize. Now I've taken care of her and managed to hurt Dorothy Lee the way you always wanted to, Mother, and I've made sure *my* daughter is never going to be second to one of the Lee girls."

"Mom?" I ask. She wouldn't have done something like that. Not to Alex's mom. Not to me.

"Don't simper, Hayes," my mom says. "I had to make a tough decision. Besides, how was I supposed to know you were in her car that day?"

"You have killed someone's child," my grandmother says. "You almost killed your own child. What were you thinking?"

"In for a penny, in for a pound," my mother says, and laughs again. "I learned that from you. Never do anything by halves. Commitment, drive, determination. Besides, it's not like you wouldn't have done this to Dorothy Lee yourself. You've hated her ever since I was a girl."

"Dorothy and I have a complicated past," my grandmother says. "You couldn't begin to understand it. But I never would have tried to balance the ledger this way. Not like this. We don't do this. There are contracts. Agreements that have existed since before you were born—"

"Those agreements can burn in hell."

"And so you called up the Gray Man?" my grandmother says. She sounds as if she's in pain.

"You would have done the same thing!"

Grandmother just stares at her.

"You took someone's mother away from her," I say. "And you almost killed me too."

"And I am so sorry," my mom's voice is gin-calm. "I made a mistake, okay? No one's perfect. And no one got hurt. I paid a terrible price, but it was worth it to protect you. To protect your future."

"How could you do this?"

All my life, I always told myself that she didn't mean to hurt me. That when she said things that cut me to the bone, they were just accidents. Mistakes, because she couldn't help herself. I never thought she'd do something like this and then act as if it were the right thing.

"Don't you see?" she says. "I want your life to be better than mine. That's all any parent wants."

"You killed my friend's mother, you tried to kill my friend, and you almost killed me!"

"And the Bailey boy," my grandmother adds, her voice dull and lifeless.

"That was a mistake. It was an accident, and it only happened once. The Gray Man got out of control, but I've reined him in. You're losing sight of what I did for Hayes."

"You're sick," I say to her. And I don't even know what to add to that, so I simply say it again. "You're sick."

Everyone is just sitting, frozen, underneath the fairy lights, and we can hear the music from the string quartet and people talking and glasses clinking, but it all just sounds like it's a long way away. No one moves. Finally, I stand up and turn to Thad.

"Come on. Madison's driving."

He and I start to go, and Madison stands up and follows. My mother catches my arm.

"You're not thinking straight," she says.

I pull my arm away, but then my grandmother is rising.

"Hayes, come with me. This is no time to rush off half-cocked. You'll sleep at my house and we'll all... we'll all talk this over in the morning."

"I'm not going anywhere with you," I say, my eyes filling with tears. "*You're* who she learned this from."

"This is a family matter. There's no need to bring outsiders into it. We can handle this within our family."

"The only family we resemble is the Mafia," I say. "Besides, you're the one who created the League. You and Dorothy. Which means Alex is my sister. And Dorothy is yours."

For the first time ever in my life, Sybil McPhillips's eyes fill with real tears. "Yes," she says. "I suppose that's true."

But I'm not listening to her anymore. I pull my arm away from my mother, and Madison, Thaddeus, and I push through the crowd and head out the door to find our friend.

21

He knows that he's not welcome here.

It's not just the simple fact that a younger man wearing a tuxedo at a social event full of people born in the fifties runs the risk of being mistaken for a waiter. He's not standing in the shadows at the back of the room so that no one else hands him an empty wineglass. He's standing in the shadows at the back of the room because he's pointedly been left off the invite list.

Deep down, most of the members of the Magnolia League assume that they're richer, better educated, and socially superior to him. Because he knows their secrets, they get nervous when they see Sam Buzzard eating at the same restaurants, watching the same movies, and buying his suits at the same stores where they shop. As soon as he's spotted at this memorial fund-raiser, it'll get back to Dorothy, and then it'll get back to Doc. But he's not missing tonight for the world. He wasn't allowed to attend Louisa's funeral, so there's no way in hell he's going to miss her memorial. He wishes he could speak, but that's impossible. So instead Sam Buzzard stands in the back of the greenhouse and listens to Dorothy Lee talk about the only woman he ever loved.

"My daughter and I had our differences," she is saying from the podium at the front of the room. "We didn't see eye to eye on some issues, but I always wanted her to grow up to be a free spirit, a free thinker, and a free woman."

Hmm, 50 percent BS, 50 percent true, Sam thinks. That's a better ratio than he'd assumed. He looks around and notices that the younger Magnolia members— Hayes, Alex, and Madison—are nowhere to be found.

"But one thing we both always agreed on was the importance of the environment," Dorothy drones on. *Why is it*, Sam wonders, *that the most fascinating, dynamic people on earth get up in front of a microphone and suddenly turn into lifeless bores?* He loved Louisa more than anyone on this planet, save her mother and her daughter, and even he has a hard time stifling his yawns.

Sam scans the room for Alex, who looks so much like Louisa that sometimes it hurts him to look at her. He's glad that she's become friends with Hayes and Madison, even if they do seem to be in some kind of a fight right now. When Louisa, Ellie, and Sandy were growing up, they didn't even bother fighting. They just ignored one another. Sandy had always been the least drunk and most sane of the three. Ellie was the lush. Anyway, Louisa was always crazy...but a wonderful kind of crazy. He misses it every day.

"I taught my daughter from an early age to respect the earth and all that grows on it," Dorothy Lee says. "And eventually her love of the green growing things that nature has to offer outstripped even my own."

Your only love of nature is what I can find in it to keep you from growing old, Sam thinks.

"I have already said enough about this memorial greenhouse," Dorothy says. "And there is someone else who knew my daughter well who would also like to say a few words. But first I'd like to share with you something I once read. The poet Douglas Malloch wrote, 'He who makes a garden works hand in hand with God.' And now, please welcome my granddaughter, Alexandria Lee."

Applause erupts in the greenhouse, sounding like warm rain falling on the roof. Sam is aware that the applause is dying out and Dorothy is still standing at the podium, her face pained. Sam looks around, like everyone else is doing, and realizes that the reason Alex isn't going to the podium is because Alex isn't here.

The applause dies out completely, and Sam feels his heart go out to Dorothy Lee. They made their peace years ago, and he knows she's humiliated up there all alone.

"Well, it looks like my granddaughter isn't available right this minute, but I'm sure she'll join us momentarily," Dorothy says. "In the meantime, please enjoy your desserts. Thank you."

Dorothy has spotted him, and her eyes are locked on his. As soon as the applause ends, Dorothy walks as directly to him as she can, stopping along the way to kiss this cheek or squeeze that hand. Then she finally reaches him.

"Here are my keys," she says, handing them to him. "Get to my house immediately and make sure Alex isn't there."

"You think she went back?"

"You've never been a fool, Sam. Don't start acting one now. Go. Right away. It will raise too many eyebrows if I leave."

"Right," Sam says, and snatches the keys from Dorothy and walks quickly out of the greenhouse.

His truck is blocked in, so he runs the ten blocks to Forsyth Park. By the time he gets there, his tuxedo is soaked through with sweat. From the outside the Lee house looks normal, but then Sam notices that the front door is open. There's a hole in the yard where someone dug up the bag of lye, the pennies and nails are missing from under the front steps, and no salt is on the threshold. Cursing softly to himself, he goes inside.

The house is dark, and his heart is in his throat as he takes the front hall stairs.

Sam has never been as comfortable with the spirit side of hoodoo as Sina has been. He considers himself a root-work man. And now, sneaking up the creaking grand staircase of Dorothy Lee's pitch-black house, Sam imagines duppies in every doorway and plat-eyes scuttling down the hall. But he's even more scared of what he's going to find in Louisa's room.

His eyes adjust enough to the darkness to let him see the Escher print torn in half and thrown on the floor. The pieces are framed in the light coming in through the windows of Louisa's room. The door is broken open, the lock smashed, the doorframe splintered.

"Louisa?" Sam calls tentatively, and then he stares into the dimness, trying to see her familiar form coalescing out of the shadows. "Are you there?"

But there's no answer. Louisa is gone. Suddenly, a lot of things slide into place all at once. It's like the pieces were in his mind all along, and he suddenly knows how they fit. Sina and Alex spending all this time together. Alex doing all this work to make the memorial happen so that everyone is out of the house. All this fighting she's done to push the other girls away. Sam's fingers feel numb and clumsy as he pulls out his cell phone and dials.

Dorothy answers instantly. "Yes?"

"Louisa's gone."

"Was it Alex?"

"She trashed the charms and broke open the seal on the room. Louisa's out there somewhere right now."

"Don't move. I'll be right there."

"No, don't," Sam says. "I know where she's going. She's gone to get Sina. They're going to give Louisa her second burial."

There is a pause.

"What is that?"

"They're putting her down."

"They cannot," Dorothy whispers fiercely. "Not without my permission."

"I'm afraid there's another way to put her to rest," Sam says. "And it's not pretty. I'll call you from the Roost." He hangs up before she can ask him any questions. Then he flies down the stairs and sprints all ten blocks to his truck.

Sina's already been responsible for the death of one child, he thinks. He's not going to let her endanger Alex too. She's always held a grudge against the Magnolia League, and she's always talked about settling old debts, ones that were run up long before she was even born. Now that Alex has put herself in Sina's hands, who knows what could happen?

Sam hits the Talmadge Bridge and leaves the bright lights of the city far behind for the dark roads out in the sea islands where the Roost lies. He hopes he's not too late. And if he is, he only has himself to blame.

When Dorothy came to him and asked him to help her bind Louisa, he'd thought she was joking. He'd known Dorothy Lee ever since he was born, and he had never known her to cry—not when her husband died, not when Louisa ran away, not when she found out she had a long-lost granddaughter. But there she was, sitting in front of him, shamefaced and weeping.

"She left me once. I can't stand to have her leave me again, you understand?"

He did understand. He'd never got to see Louisa as an adult. How she had looked when she was pregnant. How age had hardened her soft face and made her hands strong. He had missed out on her entire life after she left Savannah. He understood. He couldn't let go of her either.

And so he and Dorothy had met in secret and built the Blue Room. They had broken one of The Three and trafficked with the dead. They had dragged Louisa out of the afterlife and tied her down to the In Between. Sam had visited her constantly, always when Alex was at school. Miss Lee would leave him alone in the room, and he would talk to Louisa as if no time at all had passed.

Her spirit was a step out of time, and she seemed to be stuck in her late teens, an age when she remembered being in love with Sam. He was a familiar presence for her, and she was calm with him, a little scattered but happy, and he could usually follow the way her mind jumped around. It wasn't too much different from the way she had been in life.

One night he had sneaked back into the house when Alex was out at the Roost and Dorothy was somewhere else. The moonlight was pouring through the window like pale silver, and Louisa's spirit was almost solid, almost as if she were alive, and he had kissed her and she had kissed him back and he had forgotten that she was dead, and he had his Louisa back.

The next day he knew that this had to end. It had to end now. Before he did anything stupid or crazy or pushed things past the point where they couldn't be fixed. All he had to do was let her go, but he realized that he couldn't. Alive or dead, he would take her any way he could get her, because a world in which she had been completely erased was a world too painful for him to live in.

Sam pulls up outside the Roost and runs to Sina's house. It's dark. Privacy is always respected at the Roost, but Sam doesn't give a damn. Alex is in danger.

He lays his shoulder into Sina's front door, and it rips off its hinges and crashes to the floor.

"Sina!" he yells, but it's no use. He can tell the house is empty.

Suddenly hollow, Sam knows that he has no choice. He has to go to Doc and lay it all on the table. His sins, his errors, his violation of The Three. Doc's the only one who can help him find Sina and Alex now.

Doc's light is on, and Sam hears voices inside that suddenly stop when he knocks.

"Come," Doc calls in his heavy rumble.

Sam pushes the door open to Doc's small, cavelike house, the same one Dorothy Lee found in the country all those years ago. Sam starts talking right away. He had planned to be calm, cool, and collected, but he's too scared.

"D–Doc," he stammers, "Alex has gone missing. I think Sina may have—"

And then he freezes.

"What's the matter, Sam?" Standing behind Doc's chair, Sina smiles. "You think Sina may have what?"

"Where's Alex?" Sam asks. "What have you done with her?"

"Saved her life, from what I understand," Doc rumbles. "Earlier today we had quite a talk, and I have had revealed to me many fascinating mysteries that were hitherto hidden from my eyes. Perhaps you can shed some light on a few of the dark corners that still escape the illumination of truth, son?"

Sam has the sinking feeling that Sina has been ahead of him every step of the way and that he's just walked into a trap.

"Why don't you tell me about all this violation of The Three that's been going on, son?" Doc asks. "This disturbs me more than anything else in your sister's wild tale."

And Sam knows he doesn't have any choice but to answer.

22

Hayes

If there's one place where you really, really want the mapping app on your phone to work, it's Coachwhip Island. It's the middle of the night, and we're totally lost on the maze of dark roads out in the country. Finally, Madison pulls over to the shoulder and cuts the engine. Cicadas scream all around us in the marsh.

"We should have taken that last right," Thaddeus says from the backseat.

"We already took it!" Madison snaps.

"Maybe we should drive back to where it was familiar and, you know, start over?" I suggest.

"We have to keep going," Thad says.

"Look, we need help." I pull out my cell phone and hand it to Madison. "Here. Call Miss Lee."

"Why?"

"Because Alex is the only family she has left, and she's going to want us to keep her safe."

"Uh-uh," Madison says. "The League is the reason Alex is in trouble in the first place. It's the reason the Gray Man is on the loose. No way am I trusting any of them, especially Miss Lee."

"Thad, you know all the islands. Any clues?"

"I've never heard of Coachwhip before tonight."

"It's where Dr. Jacobs lives," Madison says.

"How do you know that?"

"I eavesdrop."

"On who?"

"God, people. On *everyone*. Y'all think I've been all about Dex lately, but the truth is I've been more checked in than any of you. I want to *leave* one day, okay? If there's a way out of here, I'm going to find it."

I think with guilt about the buzzard's rock sitting in my room. The charm that could let Madison leave anytime she wants. It's the most powerful charm the Buzzards ever made—and so far it's been entirely wasted on me.

"I wish I didn't feel like you guys are in some world that I'm not allowed to understand," Thad says.

"Don't worry about it, Thad," Madison says. "And just forget everything you hear tonight, okay? From what I'm guessing, Coachwhip is partly a real place and it's partly...I guess...not? You know. It's like a hoodoo hangout. As in, people who need to find Dr. Jacobs find it. Other people never do."

"Great," I say.

"What I'm trying to say is that it's not like you can follow directions to get there. You have to *want* to get there. And obviously we don't want to get there badly enough."

"Okay, then. Get out."

"What?"

"If what you're saying is true, then Thad needs to drive."

"Why?"

"Because he's in love with Alex."

It's blunt, and I'm sure he'll kill me for saying it, but I'm his sister and I know it's the truth. Surprisingly, however, he doesn't protest. He just takes the driver's seat, and Madison crawls into the back.

"Ugh," she moans. "I hate being demoted."

Thad pulls back out onto the road.

At first he drives hesitantly, and it feels like we're going in circles. Then he starts making turns with growing confidence and driving faster, muttering under his breath. Suddenly, there in the headlights, there's a piece of old plywood leaned up against a tree. I see the word *Coachwhip.*

"Is this a joke?" Madison asks as we take the turn way too fast. We're bouncing hard down a road that runs through the marsh, and then suddenly everything goes dark. Madison grips my hand as we hurtle into a tunnel of live oaks. Thad takes a turn way too tightly, and I can feel the thick sand causing our tires to slide.

"You wreck my car and I'll kill you," Madison says, trying to keep up a brave front.

"I've never seen this place before," Thad whispers.

The island is totally dark, silent, and completely overgrown.

"What the hell?"

Thad slams on the brakes, and Madison's car fishtails across the soft sandy track as something dark runs across the road right in front of us.

"Was that a person?" Madison asks.

"It's...a lot of people, is what it is," Thad says.

He switches off the headlights, and suddenly we can see them all around us, moving through the trees. They're everywhere—outlines of thin, stretched forms. They look like they used to be human, but now they're little more than shadows.

"Those are duppies, kids," Madison says. My heart sinks.

"Duppies?" Thaddeus whispers.

"Dead souls." Madison lowers her window. "Calling for their lost families. Listen."

The smell of salt water fills the car, and then we hear what sounds like hundreds of people crying. They're all around us, their sobs floating through the trees.

"What are they doing?"

"Usually"—Madison pauses to think—"they come out when a mother is about to lose her child."

"Or if a dead mother is about to claim one," I whisper, remembering the hoodoo story. "I mean it, Thad. Drive."

Thad starts the car again. He makes a right onto an even smaller track.

"This is seriously creepy," Madison mutters.

"We have to keep going."

We turn onto another sandy track and keep driving. Starlight filters down through the live-oak canopy as we crawl forward. Up ahead there's a strong white light shining through the trees.

"There," I say.

The engine suddenly revs up, making a horrible sound, and the car stops. Thaddeus slaps the steering wheel in frustration "We're stuck in the sand," he cries, shutting off the car. "We have to walk."

"I was afraid of that," Madison says.

"You mean because of the duppies?" I whisper.

"Yes. And also my Galliano platforms. They're going to get wrecked."

"How could we ever have dated?" Thaddeus wonders aloud.

"I rooted you, my handsome friend," Madison says, smiling.

We get out of the car. At least the sound of sobbing is starting to fade behind us. I grab Madison's and Thaddeus's hands, and we start walking over the sandy dirt toward the light.

Occasionally I see a shadow move. Up ahead I can make out Alex's Mini parked on the side of the road. The light is getting closer, while the sobs and the crying seem very far away. The wind tosses the heavy branches of the live oaks, and I could swear I hear a horse snort somewhere off in the dark trees. Finally, we reach the clearing.

"Um, Hayes," Madison says, gripping my hand so hard the circulation cuts off. We all freeze.

Lanterns hang from the trees, casting harsh white light over the ground, and in the center of the clearing there's a mound of dirt, as if someone just dug a fresh grave.

"Alex!" Thad calls, saying what we're all thinking. He sprints to the mound as if he's been prodded by ten thousand volts, then hurls himself on top of it.

"Help me!" he yells, and he's on his knees, scooping away the sand with his hands. "She's under here!"

I look at Madison. She nods, and we race over. In our dresses, we kneel down next to him in the dirt and start to dig. It's hard work, sweaty and grimy. Mosquitoes are buzzing around our heads, and sweat is staining our clothes. We're knee-deep in the hole, then waist-deep, then it's up to our necks and we're pushing dirt out as best we can, but most of it is just falling right back in.

It takes a long time, and my shoulders ache more than I ever thought possible. Dirt is everywhere: stuck to my sweat, trickling down my neckline, inside my shoes and even my underwear. Finally, after what seems like days, Thaddeus cries out in triumph.

"I've got it!" he yells, and I look where he's pointing. A small piece of pale, rough wood has emerged. "Help me get this."

He starts frantically pushing the dirt aside, and within a minute he's exposed part of what looks like a wooden lid. We try to pull it up, but it's solid. No one can seem to get a grip.

"Hang on," Madison says, and a few seconds later she's back with a tree branch the size and thickness of a crowbar.

After two false starts, Thad manages to slide it underneath the edge of the lid. As he leans on it, there's a tremendous cracking sound, and part of the lid lifts up.

"You two need to get out," he says, practically on the edge of tears. I've never seen my brother like this. Madison and I climb up out of the stifling hole.

Thad stomps on the stick again, and this time the lid lifts enough for him to get his fingers underneath it. The nails howl in protest as they're ripped up out of the wood. There's a shower of dirt, the lid lifts up higher, and finally Thad tosses it aside and we see Alex.

She's dressed in that beautiful silver-white dress, and her eyes are closed.

Thad pulls her up and, with a strangled cry, kisses her full on the lips. I can't stop staring. It's like I'm watching a scene in a movie — that's how numb I feel. She's limp in his arms, even though Thaddeus is shaking her.

"When is she going to wake up?" I hear myself ask softly. But it's not until I hear Madison weeping beside me that I really get it.

We're too late. She's dead.

23

Alex

This whole time, I thought that death was the end of everything. I was absolutely certain of it. But you know what? It's not. I'm learning that the end is just the beginning.

When I open my eyes, I see a tree. But it's not a Savannah live oak draped with moss. It's a tall, silver-trunked eucalyptus, rustling in the California breeze. It looks familiar, and after a few moments I place it.

I'm lying on my mother's favorite redwood bench, sitting up on a hill overlooking everything. I'm back at Rain Catcher Farms.

I look around. Okay, I'm not dreaming. I'm really back. I've had dreams before, and I can tell the difference—this is inarguably real. Everything is definitely in color. And I can smell it: sage and fire smoke. I pull up a blade of grass and chew it. My mouth fills with its sharp, fibrous taste. And the sounds: bamboo wind chimes clacking in the breeze; the strain of "Scarlet Begonias" drifting up from the kitchen in the Main. Below me I see Rain Catcher spread out. It's late in the day and getting dark, but only one cabin has its lights on: mine.

Feeling light-headed, I stand and walk down the hill. I don't see any people, and I start to realize that the entire camp is empty. The only sign of life comes from my cabin. I want to run to it, but I can't. The closer I get, the more wooden my legs become, until I reach the door and I'm as weak as a baby. Then I push open the screen door and step out of the darkness. And there she is. My mom.

Not dead mom, not zombie mom, but *real* mom. She's wearing the blue calico dress I saw her wearing earlier, but it's clean. Her skin is alive and brown from the sun. Her eyes are bright, and her hair is a beautiful mess. My breath catches in my chest. I've missed her so much. The enormity of her absence hits me right between the shoulder blades. Everything is suddenly too much. Then she sees me, too, and she's with me and she's wiping away wetness from my cheeks.

"Hey," she says. "Hey, don't cry, Alex. You're here now."

"Mom?" I manage, and it gets stuck in my throat and comes out like a croak.

"It's me. You brought me here. You did good, kiddo."

She takes me in her arms and I take her in mine and neither of us moves for a long time. Then, after a while, she sits back and looks at me carefully.

"What did you do to yourself?" she asks, touching my new Magnolia League hair.

I suddenly feel embarrassed and duck my head. "Nothing," I mumble.

"It's okay. It's still you in there, right?"

I nod.

"Alex, they're just a bunch of magic tricks. They're not real. You'll play with them for a while, like I did, but then you'll outgrow them. That's what's important. As long as you don't let them change who you are."

"I haven't. I'm still *me*."

"It's when you can't imagine a life without them that they get dangerous. Promise me, when you start going to the charms because you want them to *fix* you, not just to look different, promise that's when you'll stop."

"I promise," I say, but I'm not sure. Right this

minute, of course, it's easy. But I don't know if I'll be strong enough later.

"That's all that matters."

"What happened to you?" I change the subject.

"Well." She smiles. "I died."

"And this is where you've been?"

"No, sweetheart. *You* got me here, my amazing girl. Until now I've been trapped in the In Between, which is pretty much the most horrible place in the world. Or *not* in the world. And that's saying a lot for someone who lived in Cleveland in an RV once."

"But what is it?"

"It's a place where souls get unstuck in time. You can feel your body rotting, your mind falling apart, but you can't die. And you saved me from it, sugar. You brought me home."

I shake my head. I can't take it all in. "Is...anyone else here?"

"Sure. A lot of people."

"Dead people?"

"Everyone here is dead, yeah. So you don't know most of them."

"Is my dad here?"

"No," she says, going to the stove. I guess it's her turn to change the subject. "He's not."

Everything she does is familiar—filling the kettle, dumping the different herbs from their containers into the teapot, lighting the stove. I just sit there drinking her in with my eyes. There's no reason to talk. She pours the water, then brings over two chipped mugs of Swamp Brew.

"Thanks, Mom."

She sits back down cross-legged on the floor, across from me. The urge I have to touch her is a physical hunger, and I reach out and hold her hand. She smiles at me, a bit sadly.

"So what do we do now?"

"Well, that's up to you. We can go to the beach or go for a walk...."

"What? No! I want you to come back. To Life. With me."

She shakes her head. "I can't do that, sweetie. I'm dead."

"But Sina said—"

My mother's eyes widen in the old, exasperated manner. "Oh, Sina. Did she promise you that I could come back?"

"Not exactly—"

"No. She wouldn't have. She's too slippery to say anything that might trip her up. We all know that. But the dead can't come back. It's a one-way trip to the In Between, and then farther, but there's no coming back. Not unless we have special charms. Like the buzzard's rock."

"I do have it!" I say, ripping it out of the bodice of the satin dress I'm still wearing. "We can use it!"

"*One* of us can use it," she says. "And I'm not interested." She takes my hand. "What about you?"

"Well…" I look at her. Now that I'm here, I really don't think I can lose her again. "I'll stay here. I'll stay with you, and then you won't be lonely anymore. It'll just be the two of us, the way it used to be."

"You can do that," she says. "If you want."

"Yeah. It's what I want. I don't want to go back there. I want to be here with you. Nothing has to change."

"Okay," she says, getting up. She dumps her Swamp Brew into the sink and then stands with her back to me.

"What?" I ask. "What's wrong?"

Her voice isn't angry, but it sounds heavy with disappointment. "I just thought you might be the one person who could do what none of the rest of them can. I thought you could let me go. Your grandmother can't do it, and neither can Sam. They're all too good at holding on to the past, even if it's killing them."

"But then you'll be gone. I won't see you anymore."

"It happens every day, Alex. All over the world. People are here, and then they're not. Do you really want to be here in this empty place with just me? And give up everything that's back there? All of those wonderful things? Feelings? Love?"

I can't help thinking of Thaddeus.

"I don't know. I'll miss people."

"You won't, actually. Not after a while. Oh, speaking of old feelings—Reggie's here."

"Reggie? Gross! No way. Is he...?"

"Oh yes. Poor idiot. Got stoned and went surfing on the rocks one night."

"Oh," I say. First Owen, now Reggie. I feel like I'm cursed.

"Alex." My mother puts her arms around me. "Let me go while we still love each other. Don't hold on for so long that you strangle us."

"Okay." I nod. I try to be brave. Though I don't really believe I'll actually do it. "What do I do?"

"You know what to do."

"I don't."

"Just stop talking for a minute and listen."

"To what?"

"To yourself. Go outside and listen for a few minutes, and you'll know what to do."

It's hard to walk away after missing her for so long, but she's staring at me like I have to, so I walk outside. I sit on the front steps of our cabin and look out over the farm as night creeps in. The sun's just dropped behind the hills, and we're in the mouth of the evening, when the long shadows melt and the air goes gray. I close my eyes.

Maybe it's the hours of reading books about hoodoo, or something Sina told me, or the sound of the eucalyptus leaves. Because finally it comes to me that what's important isn't what I have, or how I look, or my friends, or the League, or anything. It's my blood, running from me back to my mother and then back to my grandmother and back to her mother and on back to the beginning. It's a river, and if I'm quiet, it sings in my ears and tells me what to do.

After a while, I open my eyes, and people are there, all around me. A lot of them are strangers. But then I spot Big Jon and...Reggie.

"Hey, Alex!" Big Jon booms.

"Big Jon?" I say, blinking. "Did you—?"

"Heart attack." He smiles, shaking his head. "After all that damned vegan food, I bit it in my hot tub."

"Reggie?" I turn and look at my ex. Though it's hard to believe I ever liked him. He's so skinny— almost skeletal. And even now, his eyes are too shifty to trust. "Heard about what happened. I'm really sorry."

He shrugs. "Just wish I'd gotten Crystal to come surfing with me. This place gets boring, Pudge. Not enough sex."

"Right." Even in the afterlife, he's still a total jerk.

"So, Alex," Big Jon says, "we're hangin' in the Main. Wanna come?"

"In a minute."

"Actually, I gotta talk to her," Reggie says. "Catch up in a bit, okay?"

Big Jon waves and disappears down the path to the

Main. Reggie sits down on the steps next to me, and I wince. I still can't believe I liked this creep. But I really don't want to be stuck talking to him in . . . well, wherever we are.

"So, Pudge . . ."

"Don't call me that."

"It's just a nickname. I don't mean anything by it."

"It's not my name."

I slide far away from him, but he doesn't go away.

"I'm sorry, Alex. For what I did to you."

"It's fine. I'm really, really over it."

"Good, good. Hey, can I talk to you? Away from here?"

"No."

"It's about your mom."

I look up at the cabin, where my mom is still moving around inside.

"What about her?"

"Well, I stole something from her."

"What?" I ask, suddenly realizing, with a sinking feeling, that it all fits.

"Just some necklace. I got hired by some old chick who put an ad on Craigslist. Pretty hot, actually. Southern. Before I knew you. She paid my way here and stuff, and all I had to do was—"

"Steal my mom's necklace."

"Yeah. Well, not steal it. But take it off her neck. So while she was sleeping—"

"You took it. Then you threw it away in the garden."

"Yeah. So it wasn't really stealing. I just tossed it. But I've always felt bad about that. I knew it was a bizarre thing to do, and I guess I knew something was wrong."

"But you weren't at the RC then," I say, shaking my head. "That makes no sense."

"Well, you're right. I only came back after the job. The place looked cool... and the topless chicks..."

"Ugh. Please stop talking." It was definitely wrong, what he did. He helped kill my mother. But it's done. And in this place, where everything feels sort of flat, old business like this doesn't seem to matter anymore.

We sit in silence for a while as he rubs his palms together. "You sticking around?"

"I don't know. I have something important to do."

"Hang out with your dad?"

"What?" This guy is dumber than I ever knew. Even dead. "You know I've never met my dad."

My mom comes out, and Reggie slinks into the shadows. People are playing Ultimate Frisbee and Hacky Sack all around. It's like I remember it, but something's different. It's as if there's a film over everything. I don't feel happy or sad. I just *am*.

"There's something weird about all this."

"I told you," Mom says. "No feelings."

"What does that mean, exactly?"

"There are no feelings here," my mother says. "We're dead."

"Right." I look around. It's true. I feel content but not joyful, the way I used to when I lived here. I'm annoyed but not disgusted by how horrible Reggie's been.

"But *you*'re not dead," she says. "Not yet."

"That's why I still love you."

"Probably not just me," she says, smiling.

Immediately, I think of Thaddeus.

"I must not be totally dead yet," I say, grinning. "Because, yeah, I still feel something."

"I can see that. Your love vibes are harshing our numb zazen trip."

I laugh. Then... I remember. "I need to go to the In Between first."

She looks at me curiously. "What?"

"I need to go talk to someone. Strike a deal."

"Who?"

"The Gray Man."

She shakes her head. "Honey, there's nothing you can do about him."

"I don't believe that."

"You have to. He's not a person. He never was. He was a monster in life, and now that he's half dead, he's even worse."

"He took the most precious person in the world away from me," I say, my voice growing thicker.

"No," she says. "Ellie did that."

"Ellie? Sybil's—"

"There's a story, honey. But it's over now."

"I'll—" My head is buzzing. But I know that time is running out. It's getting harder to hold on to thoughts and feelings, and anything I feel about Ellie slips out of my mind like a soap bubble. "Mom, he has to be dealt with."

"He's stronger than you are," she says calmly.

It's true what she said about being dead. She really can't feel anything. Otherwise she'd be yelling at me, not speaking to me in this reasonable tone.

"I think I can make him an offer he can't refuse," I say, but it sounds a whole lot tougher than I feel.

She looks out over the field. "You can't do anything about him; just let him get bored. He'll go away eventually. Move on to some other people."

"Mom, why is that a good solution? How many people will he kill? He's already killed a boy who... who wasn't a great guy, but he deserved to grow up. He deserved to live. He shouldn't have died alone and scared."

She shakes her head. "That's not your problem, Alex. You can't bring that boy back."

"It is my problem, Mom. Or else I've changed into someone I don't know anymore."

"I..." she starts, and then trails off.

"I have the buzzard's rock. I'm not scared." Which is a lie.

"Do you know what you have to do?"

I know. Without knowing how, I know. I nod.

"What can I say to make you go home and keep yourself safe?"

"I couldn't live with myself if I did that. I'm the only one with a shot at stopping this thing."

She smiles sadly and then kisses my cheek.

"Will I ever see you again?"

"If you need to," she says. "I'm your spirit sister. When you call, I'll come, but don't make a habit of it. I'm part of your past, and you need to have your own life now."

"It's not fair."

"I know it's not fair. But it's life."

"Well, then life sucks."

"No, it doesn't," she says. "Not when you consider the alternatives."

We've reached the gate into the Sanctuary. Inside, a mist has risen, and the plants are just dim shapes, half hidden. Mom stops and hugs me.

"Are you ready?"

"Not really."

"You don't have to do this."

"I do."

I hug her again.

"I love you, Mom."

"Then it's time to let me go."

I turn and walk away, leaving her by the Sanctuary.

I hold her hand until the last minute. I have to literally tear my fingers from hers, that's how much it hurts. Then I go away forever. At the bottom of the path, her blue 1973 VW bus is waiting. In Life, at this point, the van is no more than a pile of rust in a junkyard somewhere in Ukiah. But here it's exactly the way I remember it, and the keys are in the ignition.

I get in, crank her up, and gun it. The engine roars, and I drive in the waning dusk, heading up into the hairpin curves of Orr Springs Road. Then, after about eighteen miles, I close my eyes, jerk the wheel to the left, and drive off the highest cliff I can find.

24

They think they've bested him. These Savannah women, these slip-skins, with their duppies and their hoodoo doctors. But what William Long knows is that no one has the power to get rid of him for good. No one's immortal, but he's the closest thing there is. He's stronger than death. Stronger than all of them.

Even the one who conjured him has come begging him to stop. She came, groveling, to their meeting place at the old Execution Tree after she was found out. Drunk, as usual, and loaded down with whiskey, raw chicken, and chocolate.

"Please leave Alex alone," she whined. "They're catching on to me." Of course, he's not interested in Alexandria anymore. She's too troublesome. It's the blonde he wants now. On the ship they would have called her "perfect gold." Innocent. Skin as white as ivory. In his day, that girl would have been the most sought-after conquest, until there was no use for her anymore.

He's been tracking her for days, waiting to make her his puppet, taste life through her eyes, then drag her down to the In Between to be his bride for as long as she lasts. After all, he's been thinking that marriage might suit a man of his stature now.

The first one he'll have her kill for him is that skinny Buzzard woman. How dare she trick him out of that girl's body? He had the right to be there; the law of the crossroads was on his side. And then...well, once that one's gone, he'll have her kill the old man, the Buzzard father. And then...well. He'll have to see.

He stands among the trees of Coachwhip, hidden inside the In Between. The half-dead place is pulled around him like a black shadow, and he holds stolen eyes in his hand and uses them to watch the beautiful girl cry over some trivial thing—hiding her face, all full of guilt and remorse.

Dr. Jacobs has done fair work tonight, freeing the

Magnolia woman from the In Between and sending her on into death with the help of the scrawny Buzzard slip-skin. He's relieved, frankly. When he had taken her, he hadn't expected she'd stay in the In Between for so long. It annoyed him. She was easily hurt, easily scared, not at all suited for his kingdom. He prefers them a little bit guilty, a little bit conflicted, a little bit ashamed. And it made him happy that to free the dead woman's soul, they had to kill her daughter. Clumsiness always amuses him.

"William Long." He hears a familiar voice behind him. He turns his stolen eyes into the shifting shadows of the In Between. They show him a face he thought was dead and buried.

What do you want, girl? he growls. *You should be gone. They buried your husk. Somebody curse you?*

"I'm here by choice," Alex says in a steady voice.

Not for long, he snarls. *Nobody but me stands it for long.*

"You're a murdering piece of trash," the girl says. "You couldn't make an honest living, could you? So you stole from others."

So long ago, I can't remember. I'm two hundred and something years old, witchling. I am the king of the In Between, the emperor of un-Life. Bow down, show me respect, and I may ease your passage.

"You're nothing. A killer, long forgotten. Nobody but the Buzzards remembers you," she says. "Maybe one drunk old lady who called you up with her own blood."

He starts forward. *I'm going to tear you to pieces right now.*

"You caaa-an't," she says, in a singsong voice. Then she holds up the necklace.

With rage, he feels himself weaken. Her mother had it before — it kept him from taking her away. For years he watched for his moment to strike, and all that time his uncompleted task galled him, like something stuck between his teeth. He has developed a hatred and fear of the rock.

You get away from me, he says. *You may be protected, but your friends are not.*

"You stay away from them, or I'll come looking for you. Not feeling very well, are you? The charm too much for you?"

I'll—

"You think you're brave? Killing kids on the road?"

Need their eyes.

"My friends," Alex says. "They are protected."

By whom?

She seems to waver. But then she holds up the rock again. "By me."

You?

"As long as they stay in Savannah. All the Magnolias are under my protection."

He grits his rotting black teeth.

You're their new nursemaid?

"I'm in charge of the Magnolia League. I've vowed to uphold its compacts and secrets. And I will kill you if you come near any of them."

What about the conjurer? The one who rooted your mama? You're going to protect her too? Why not leave her for me? I need fresh eyes.

The girl thinks about his request a moment. "I don't bargain with the dead. All the Magnolias are under my protection. And their families too. As long as they stay in this city."

He growls. *You have to strike a bargain with me, puppy. You say you protect them if I don't kill, but what do I get? What does your protection mean to me?*

"Means daily bowls of whiskey. Means two raw chickens a day. Means cow eyes, when we can get them. As long as you leave the Savannah Magnolias alone."

He uses the dead boy's eyes to peer through the thick blackness of the In Between at the group gathered around the grave. Then he subtly turns one eye so it can show him again the blonde hiding and watching them, and then she stands up and slips away from the light and into the darkness.

So this is your deal with the dead? he growls. *Then I swear to you as the head of your clan. As long as your people stay in Savannah, they're under the rock.*

"Good. And I promise in return to keep the offerings coming to you, to help take the bite off your hunger."

He can't help smiling. He knows where the blonde one he wants is going. And that means, even with his bargain, he can have exactly what he wants.

"I just need you to do one more thing for me," the girl says.

Which is?

"Kill me back to life."

Gladly, he answers. Then, with his old sword, he swiftly grants her wish. The shock of it, the raw pain as it tears through her chest, pushes her back through the shadows, and she feels the air thicken and ripple around her and color return to the world as she falls out of the In Between and back into Life.

25

Hayes

Before Alex started breathing again, we'd thought she was dead for almost half an hour. Madison and I watched, speechless, as my brother hauled her limp body to the edge of the hole we'd dug.

"Help," he barked.

We both jumped a little, as if jolted out of our individual bad dreams, and grabbed her under the arms. She was as heavy as a corpse and, inelegantly, we wrestled her up onto the ground. I rolled her onto her back and stopped when I saw her face. It was lifeless, like it was made of plastic. There was dirt in her eyes and mouth.

Madison pushed me aside and leaned over Alex. She felt Alex's throat and then her wrist, put an ear to her chest. Then Madison shook her head.

That's when I ran for the trees. It's not that I don't love Alex, and it's not that I didn't want to try to help her, but I just couldn't watch anymore. I couldn't live with myself if I'd made the vision come true. I hid behind a pine about twenty feet away, listening.

"Move," Thad barked.

"We have to call nine-one-one," Madison said.

"She's going to be all right."

"Thad, she's—"

"She's going to be fine."

I peeked out to watch them. He placed his hands, one cupped over the other, on her chest and then slammed them down, compressing her chest three times, counting out loud and then checking her breath, then pushing down on her chest again. He felt inside her mouth with black fingers and bent over her, pressed his lips to hers, and blew three times. I always thought mouth-to-mouth would be sort of romantic, but in reality it's brutal, like he's attacking her, or fighting her body to keep her alive.

And then, finally, Alex coughed and retched. Thad rolled her over onto her side. When she stopped gagging, she turned her head and saw him looking at her.

"Hi, Thaddeus," she said. She was definitely alive. And she was laughing.

"Not that I usually stoop to common profanity," Madison said, "but thank fucking God."

She's alive. My friend is *alive*. I want to be with them, to celebrate. But I feel positively sick inside. I'm the reason this happened. My mom, my grandmother, me—the three of us almost killed Alex.

I could go and apologize, of course, and they'd probably all pretend to forgive me. But the fact is, I'll always be the one whose mother did this. I'll always be poisoned by my blood. So even though it's nice to think life could go back to normal, normal isn't what I want anymore. Normal means I grow up to be like my grandmother and my mother. While I'll never stop loving them, I don't want to be them. Ever.

I think about saying good-bye, but Thaddeus and Alex are too busy making out to notice anything, and what would I say, anyway? So I slip away. Madison's back is to me, and I walk up the road to where Alex's car is parked just out of range of the lantern light. I know it's dramatic to leave like this, but it's been a dramatic evening. And when you decide to change your life, you usually want to get started as soon as possible.

Alex's purse, with her keys inside it, is on the floor

of the passenger side. I take them out, turn the ignition, make a U-turn, and leave Coachwhip Island.

Never in a million years would I have thought I'd be the one to leave Savannah. Yet there are things that are broken now that can never be repaired. Of course, some things were always broken, but I just never noticed them before. I was too happy with the way life was going for me. Had Alex not come into our lives, I would have been on the fast track to becoming just like my mother and my grandmother, using other people to get what I want. Possibly killing them. I would have been rich, but I don't think I would have been alive. Not really. Not in any way that counts.

I park up the road from the Buzzard's Roost, just as I've done so many times before. Only this time no one can know that I'm coming. I get out of my car and walk down the road, acorns crunching under the soles of my shoes. Climbing the gate as gracelessly as ever, I make my way toward the garden.

It's completely dark out. I can hear voices from the common building, where people are having dinner or maybe a party. On another day that might have made me feel a little lonely, but I'm just glad they're not going to hear what I'm doing until it's too late.

The door to Doc's private shed in the back of the garden isn't locked. I push it open without a sound, my heart pounding loudly. It takes me a little time, using the light on my cell phone, to illuminate the crowded wall of strange-looking books and albums, but finally I find the one with markings on the spine that I recognize. It's a weird series of scratches, not proper writing at all, really, but I had a little bracelet I wore until first grade that had the same illegible writing on it. I'd recognize the scratches anywhere. I pull the book down and begin flipping through the damp pages.

I knew this thing existed, but now that it's in my hands, it's hard to digest. The book is full of *me*. Locks of my hair. A vellum envelope with my baby teeth inside. Charms and sigils. Talismans and scraps of paper. Tests I took when I was in fourth grade. Certificates of achievement. Prescriptions for curing harm and preventing illness. I look at all the other books lining the shelves, all with different markings on the spine. One for Madison. Another one, thin, for Alex. These are the books of the Magnolia League, living and dead.

I take a deep breath, pour my baby teeth into a mortar, and use a pestle to grind them into dust, which I scatter on the dirt floor. Then I put the book on a millstone sunk in the dirt floor and tear out the pages, crumpling them up. Next I pile my locks of hair on top, and then the discarded covers of the book go in the pile. Finally, I take the box of matches from the altar in the corner.

I pause. I know that when I do this, I'll lose everything. Every plan my mother and grandmother ever made for me. No Magnolia League. No roots, no conjure, no status, no power, no protection. Just me, starting over with nothing but my name.

I light a match and put the flame to the pile of charms.

My name is Hayes Mary McCord Anderson. And I'm free.

26

Alex

It's taken us an hour to get the car out of the sand. It didn't help that Thaddeus kept pulling me aside and kissing me, but I figure he deserves it, after digging me up. Finally, we stick branches under the tires and, with a spray of sand, the car lurches free.

"Let's go," Madison shouts. Ever since Hayes disappeared with my Mini, Madison's been desperate to find her.

The sun's already coming up, and the sky is turning a hazy gray. We get in the car and Thaddeus drives. Madison is too stressed out to be behind the wheel. Making our way out of the marsh, we pull onto the two-lane country road leading back to Savannah. All of us check our cell phones, and then Thad stops, staring at his.

"Eyes on the road," I say.

"Here." He hands his phone to Madison.

She listens and then hangs up. "So that's it?"

"I guess so," Thaddeus says.

"What happened?" I ask.

"Hayes left a message—she's leaving town for a while," Madison says. "You know, I think she couldn't have come up with a better idea. I can say she's at my house and tell my mom she's back home. That'll buy her a few hours."

"Good," Thaddeus says. "It'll be good for her."

"Wait," I say, adrenaline suddenly flooding my veins. "What? How'd she get out of Savannah? And what about the Blue Root?"

"She has the buzzard's rock," Madison says.

"No," I say, my voice rising. "She doesn't."

"What?"

"I took it," I say, tearing the necklace out of my filthy bodice. "I used it to cut a deal with the Gray Man."

"What?" Madison yells.

"Alex, what? How'd you see him? Much less *talk* to him?" Thaddeus asks.

"Let's just say I took a journey. And that I'm really glad to be back."

"But why did you do that to Hayes? You stole the rock?"

I shake my head. "I didn't mean to hurt her. I switched it. At the time, she was under the Gray Man's influence. He had turned her against me, and she wouldn't have understood."

"Oh my God," Madison says. "So not only does she have a Blue Root to deal with—"

"But the Gray Man is probably after her too."

"Is this bad?" Thaddeus asks, his voice shaking with alarm.

"It's the worst," I answer.

"We have to do something," Thaddeus says. "That's my sister out there!"

"There's only one thing to do," Madison says grimly. "Call the Magnolias. Now."

27

Alex

Magnolia League Meeting, Number 450
Miss Lee presiding
Refreshments: none

You can tell things are serious, because normally at a Magnolia League meeting there are refreshments — white wine, tea, and always something to eat. This morning, though, there's nothing but three big pitchers of ice water. No one seems to have slept last night after the greenhouse dedication spectacularly self-destructed, and I can tell everyone's dying for some coffee, but no one dares to ask. The air feels thick with tension.

My grandmother, dressed somberly in a dark pantsuit, hasn't spoken to me all morning. Sybil McPhillips and Ellie Anderson are sitting next to each other across the table from Dorothy. Sybil looks like she's been crying; Ellie looks like she's still drunk. The rest of the Senior Four, Mary Oglethorpe and Khaki Pettit, are already seated, trying to process what they've heard. Madison and I take our places with the other lesser members, bracing for the storm that's coming.

"Ladies," Dorothy begins, "you all know why we're here."

"We *do*!" Sybil bursts out. "Where is my granddaughter? Who let her run away? I am just about ready to *sue* someone over this!"

"You're not the only one," my grandmother says. "But rest assured, sister, we will find Hayes. And we will find out what happened last night."

"I want my daughter back!" Ellie cries.

"Do shut up, Ellie." My grandmother sighs. "I am very fond of your daughter, but it's your stupidity that got her taken in the first place."

"Hayes doesn't deserve to pay for her mother's mistake," Khaki says.

"Which is why we are checking our armory," my

grandmother says. "And why we've called a special guest."

"Guest?" Sybil asks.

Miss Lee rises and walks over to the heavy sliding door on the far side of the room. With a strong tug, she pulls it open. A man in a blue silk jacket is sitting cross-legged in a velvet chair. He waits patiently, a half smile on his face, wearing sunglasses with blue mirrored lenses, dress pants, and crocodile shoes. His face is ancient and wizened, his skin the texture of tree bark.

The ladies murmur in surprise. A few rise.

"What is *he* doing here?" Sybil demands.

"I'm not happy about it either," my grandmother replies. She turns to Doc Buzzard. "But in some ways he is our founder, and he called this meeting even before Madison phoned me this morning. Doctor?"

Doc Buzzard surveys the room with a princely gaze. He uncrosses and recrosses his legs, drumming his fingers on the arms of the chair.

"My daughter will be joining us," he says.

There's a collective wave of disapproval at this news. Sina has never joined a Magnolia event, and the older members are particularly suspicious of her.

"Doc," my grandmother says, "we can't let a slip-skin into this house."

"You don't get to choose who comes into this house anymore." Doc Buzzard turns to me. "Go bring my daughter in," he commands.

I look to my grandmother, but she offers no help. No one will meet my eyes, and so finally I go downstairs to the front door. I open it and Sina is waiting. She brushes past me and takes the stairs, two at a time. I race after her. When I get back, she's standing behind her father's chair.

Only Ellie is stupid enough to talk.

"*Where* is Hayes? What have you done with her? I've half a mind to call the police!"

"Your daughter is very lucky she's not dead," Doc says calmly. "And she would be creepin' to Jesus right this minute if it wasn't for my Sina. So a little bit of gratitude wouldn't be out of place."

"I'm sorry," Khaki says, lowering her tortoiseshell glasses in order to get a better look at Doc Buzzard. "Our children have been attacked by a man who has been dead for over a century. Forgive us for not writing a thank-you note to Sina."

"Sina didn't raise him up," Doc says. "And she doesn't expect your thanks. Just like we don't expect anything from any of you every time we do you a root or make a good turn for you. Just like every time we get one of your husbands reelected or make sure one of your investments goes up, or your business dealings go smooth, or your grandchildren grow up healthy. We don't ever expect to hear 'thank you.' And that's all right. We've gotten used to your manners by now."

"We're not here to keep score, Doctor," my

grandmother says. "Our gratitude goes without saying. And certainly our money speaks louder than words. So now, please, get to the point."

Doc puts his hands on his knees and leans forward.

"The point? Well, the point is that I am very angry with every single one of you," he says. "Sina, explain to these women how they've crossed me."

"Dr. Jacobs is seeing patients again," she says. "The road to Coachwhip Island has been reopened. He's the one who called up the Gray Man, but he did it for money that one of you paid him."

"If you're suggesting I had anything to do with that," Hayes's mother says, raising her hand to her chest, "I would remind you that *I'm* the one who's lost a child here."

"Because you're thicker than mud," Doc Buzzard says. "Because you let the Gray Man get a taste of your blood when you pulled him out of the In Between, and now he's hungry for it again. And while you are a very well-protected woman, your daughter is not. He can't slake his thirst on you, so he'll take someone younger and fresher. Sina, tell these nice ladies the rest."

Sina puts her hands on her hips, surveying the room dramatically. "The Gray Man's been raised, the future's been seen, sister has gone against sister, and you've had truck with the dead. The Three haven't just been broken; they've been smashed to bits."

She glances quickly at me. I see the ghost of a smile

flit across her lips, and a sick realization washes over me. I know how I held up Sina's part of the bargain. How I've destroyed the Magnolia League. I wanted my mother back so badly that I didn't even notice that Sina was using me as a pawn to get everyone to break The Three.

"If someone's gone to Dr. Jacobs," my grandmother says, "then she must be dealt with."

"That's right," Doc Buzzard agrees. "Sina, give Miss Dorothy the names of these oath breakers."

"Alexandria Lee's gone to Dr. Jacobs to have truck with the dead," Sina says. I feel my heart sink. "But not before her grandmother trafficked with the dead by staking down Louisa Lee's spirit."

"Miss Dorothy," Doc Buzzard says. "I'm surprised you managed that on your own. Surprised and disappointed."

"I didn't," my grandmother says. "I had help. Your son Sam, in fact."

"Ah, well. Sam had his reasons. We know that."

What is he talking about?

"I'll address his failings in good time. Daughter, do continue."

"Ellie Anderson's gone to Dr. Jacobs to call up the Gray Man and set him on a sister," Sina says. "Khaki Pettit helped her granddaughter and Sybil's granddaughter see the future. They've all broken The Three."

"You're just a nasty old nest of vipers, aren't you?" Doc Buzzard says.

"I suppose each of us did what she thought she had to do," my grandmother says.

"I'm sure you did," Doc Buzzard says. "So let me tell you this: The Magnolia League is finished. I'm closing it down. I'm taking back all my charms and roots. As of this minute, you are officially defunct."

"You can't do that!"

"I *can* do that, Dorothy. And I can do worse if I've got a mind to. You want me to do worse?"

"I don't care," Ellie says. "I don't care what you do. *I'm* going to find my daughter."

"I don't think so, Ellie," Doc Buzzard says. "I'm taking back all my root work, but one charm is staying: the Blue Root. I'm leaving it up, so anyone who leaves Savannah will be having a very short trip."

"You can't do this!" Ellie cries.

"My granddaughter is out there," Sybil says through clenched teeth. "I need to bring her home."

"Why? She's done us a favor," Doc Buzzard says. "She's lured the Gray Man away with her. Now all we have to deal with here is Dr. Jacobs. After we've taken him in hand, we can turn our attention to your granddaughter."

"He isn't after her now?" Ellie asks. "Is he?"

"Don't worry," Doc Buzzard says. "You don't deserve this comfort, but you may as well know she's got the buzzard's rock. He can't hurt her as long as she's got that."

Ice water runs down my spine.

"Thank goodness," Sybil says. "As awful as you are, Alex, thank goodness you gave Hayes the stone."

"You will stay in Savannah until further notice," Doc Buzzard says. "I'm keeping y'all on a short leash. I'll leave you with your personal charms because I wouldn't want you nice ladies to scare the horses by suddenly looking your age. But all the conjures you have for money and wealth, for personal power and for luck in business, for your children's schools and for your yards and cars, I'm taking those away."

"How long will this last?" Mary Oglethorpe asks.

"Until I say so."

"Very well, Doctor," my grandmother finally says. "We'll do as you say."

Doc Buzzard's face splits into an enormous grin.

"I don't care why you do it, Dorothy," he says, then stands. "Because you don't have a choice. This building is closed until further notice. Now all of you scat. And don't none of you worry yourselves any: I'll give you a discount on your bill for this interruption in services."

And with that, he's finished with us. Sina leads everyone downstairs and out the front door, and just like that—we're banished from 404 Habersham. We all file outside in a large, well-dressed swarm and mill about on the sidewalk. No one's quite sure what to do with herself.

"Well," Sybil says to my grandmother, "here we are again."

"Yes," my grandmother replies. "Naturally, just as when we were sixteen, I believe this is completely your fault."

"And I you."

The other Magnolias stand by silently as the two women look at each other like pregnant cats in July.

"Well. No use fighting now."

"True."

"You still have some Black Heart charm in you?" Dorothy asks.

"Fresh as ever," Sybil says. "You still remember how to conjure a few Fallen Ladies and a zombie death?"

"A real woman never loses her touch."

"Hang on," I say. "You guys practiced hoodoo *before* the Magnolia League?"

"Dear. Please say '*y'all*' in these circumstances. No Southern lady will take you seriously if you call her a 'guy.' The word is not just about laziness. It's about addressing groups *properly*. And, yes, Sybil and I knew a bit of hoodoo before we contacted the Buzzards."

"But I thought you first learned about the magic because your boyfriend's dad was cursed."

"Her boyfriend's dad didn't want him marrying a lowlife like Dorothy," Sybil says. "So *she* cursed *him*."

"Not before *you* used conjure to steal my boyfriend away."

"Wait, Senator McPhillips is..."

"He was better-looking then," my grandmother says.

"So that whole story wasn't true?"

"Oh, don't be so righteous. Everyone has her own truths," Sybil says. "We started the League because we were in over our heads. We needed Doc's help to clean up our mess. That's the short version, naturally, but the point is, we have a teensy bit of magic we learned from our own mothers and nannies. And we're going to have to scrape it together and use it."

"I am willing to take steps if that is what's necessary," Dorothy says haughtily.

"We need to meet privately to inventory our supplies." Sybil matches my grandmother's icy tone.

"And," Dorothy continues, her voice becoming louder so as not to be overshadowed, "we need to ascertain whether we have any Buzzards who will go against Doc and work with us."

"I believe you already have one," Sybil says.

"What do you—?"

"Alex," Madison says, grabbing my arm. "We've got to go. Seriously. Right this second."

"Yes," my grandmother says quickly. "Do run along."

"Okay," I say. "Good luck with your... plotting."

"Magnolias don't need luck," Sybil says. "We make it for ourselves."

"Right," I say. Then, head still spinning, I run up the street after Madison.

I haven't even had time for a shower since coming back from the dead, but Madison drags me straight into Leopold's Ice Cream. Judging by the look on the counter jockey's face, he has never seen a girl in a satin dress covered in graveyard dirt before.

"Looks like it was a hell of a party," he says, handing us our chocolate nut sundaes.

"You have no idea," I say.

"Okay," Madison says once we've tucked into our mountains of ice cream. "I think I know where she went."

"Where? Because this is beyond bad."

"The one place in North America where they worship the French as much as Hayes does?"

"Um...Montreal?"

"I'm going to pretend you didn't say that. *Canada?* No. She's gone to New Orleans. The French Quarter, most likely. She's been obsessing about France since we were kids, but I don't think she's got it in her to head for Europe the first time out. That's the next best place."

"Okay!" I cry, relieved. "So which of us is going?"

She looks at me blankly. "What do you mean? We'll go together."

"Mad, there's only *one* buzzard's rock."

"So?" Madison shakes her head. "We'll break it in

half. Or each of us wears it half the time or something. I am not doing this without you."

I reach over and grab her hand. "Madison, you're her best friend. I'll cover for you and buy you time to get out of here, but you have to go. Now. The Gray Man could be on her right this minute, sniffing her out, tracking her down. An hour's delay might be too late."

"I can't believe you're putting this on me," she shrieks, ripping her hand away and throwing down her spoon. Other early-morning sugar junkies turn their heads curiously to see what's going on.

"Listen to me," I whisper. "You're the only one who can do this. You're the only one who can bring Hayes home."

Madison picks up her spoon and quietly eats her ice cream. Finally, she licks all the fudge off the bottom of the bowl and puts it down.

"Tell Dex I'll call him," she says. "And cover for me until at least tomorrow morning."

"No problem."

"And give me all your cash. If I use my card, they'll be able to track me."

"Sure." I empty my wallet, then hand her the envelope containing the five hundred dollars Constance Taylor gave me what seems like a lifetime ago. I've had it in my purse ever since the Christmas Ball.

"All right," Madison says, counting. "That'll at least get me a tank of premium."

"Okay...and here." I turn away from her, then pull the buzzard's rock out of my dress and tuck it into a silk bag on a long string. Reluctantly, Madison takes it, puts it around her neck, and drops it inside her shirt. We walk back outside to where her car is parked—illegally, of course.

"I've got to say," she grumbles as she gets in, "I liked the way things were around here a whole lot more before you showed up."

"But now you get to leave. It's what you wanted, right?"

"I meant design school at Parsons. Not chasing some phantom killer to New Orleans to save my best friend's life."

"You scared?"

"Am I scared?" Madison turns the words over, considering this. "Yeah, I'm scared. I'm scared I won't find her, or that she's already dead."

"Don't say that."

"There's nothing wrong with facing facts. Not enough people around here do that." She tosses her long hair defiantly. "But I'm not worried. If you can die and come back, I can get Hayes away from the Gray Man."

"Right." We smile at each other a little sadly. I think how much life has changed for Hayes and Madison. A year ago, things were so simple for them: boys, parties, friends, clothes. But then Hayes's mother killed my mother out of petty jealousy and spite, and this war began.

Because hoodoo isn't just about staying young and rich. Nothing so coveted could come so easily. The magic draws its power from death. And when you raise the stakes that high, the outcome isn't pretty.

"Good luck."

"MGs don't need luck," Madison says. "Didn't you hear Sybil? We make our own."

"Yeah," I say. "I hope she's right."

And then Madison floors it. But before her car turns the corner, I catch a glimpse of her pale face in the rearview mirror. She looks terrified, and I can't blame her.

We're in danger, all of us. It's not just Hayes. The Magnolias have lost everything—our charms, our protections, our trust in one another. Who knows how many plat-eyes, curses, and old Blue Roots have been set loose? The good life is over, that's for certain. Sina got exactly what she wanted. But now the rest of us have to band together, gather our charms, and come up with one final, seriously kick-ass hoodoo party. Call it the Final Ball if you want—as long as we manage to come out of it alive.

EXCERPTS FROM

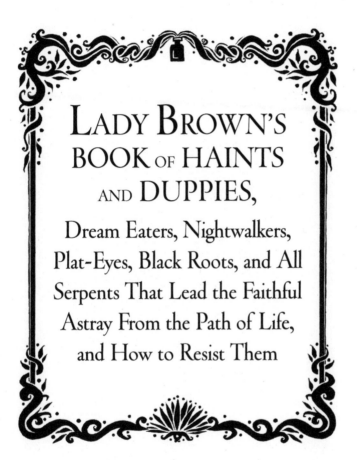

LADY BROWN'S BOOK OF HAINTS AND DUPPIES,

Dream Eaters, Nightwalkers, Plat-Eyes, Black Roots, and All Serpents That Lead the Faithful Astray From the Path of Life, and How to Resist Them

GHOST LIGHTS

There are many snares to lead good people astray when they venture out walking late at night, but the worst is the ghost light. The ghost light is what remains of a person who was lost and wandered until hunger and thirst overcame him and he took to the grave. His lonely bones rot in some secret hiding place, and in his solitude he seeks out companions. To trick travelers, this spirit sets his head alight and burns with a cold green fire that appears to be the light of a friendly house or a lantern offering guidance to those who are lost in the dark. The ghost light seeks to deceive you and to lead you into darkness, where you will step into a swamp or a creek. The spirit will hold you under the water until you join him, adding another light to his.

To avoid ghost lights, it is best not to go walking late at night in unfamiliar places. If your business requires that you do, then keep your eyes on your feet and do not look up, or you will be led astray. It is helpful to recite the Lord's Prayer one dozen times before walking into the night. This will not disturb the ghost lights, but it will bring comfort to the traveler.

OLD LOVES, SAY GOOD-BYE

Sometimes old loves caught in the In Between want to say good-bye. Saying good-bye is a loving and healthy thing, but many old loves have bad memories and may want to say good-bye over and over, haunting you.

To prevent mothers and fathers and aunts from saying good-bye to children, pass the children over the grave at the burial three times. If a dead lover is saying good-bye over and over, take a piece of clothing that smells like you and put it on your closed door at night. That should be enough of you so that she doesn't wake you up. *Never* encourage a dead lover to visit. It may seem like a good idea if you miss someone, but you will be sorry, especially when you find a new love and the old one is still there. If the clothes trick is not working and you are with a new lover, sprinkle pepper and your tears outside your door. Pepper will warm the dead lover, which is part of what she's looking for, but your tears are what she really wants if you are with someone new. If she has a vial of them, she will be satisfied and will go away for a while.

GRAY MAN AT THE CROSSROADS

When you are looking to truck and bargain with devils and nightwalkers, you must venture down to the crossroads. This is a place of power because it is everywhere and it is nowhere all at once. The crossroads is not here, nor is it over there. It is not east, or north, or west, or south. It is halfway on the journey, and it lies just outside of town. The crossroads is the place all men and all devils must pass through as they move from one place to another. If you are looking to make a bargain or strike a deal with a nightwalker, the crossroads is where you must go.

Take what it is you're wanting and find a crossroads far from town where you will not be disturbed. Go out there for nine nights in a row. Arrive at midnight and stand in the middle of the crossroads. Then turn and face each of the roads, one by one, and recite nine times, "Come to me, and teach me." Do not wash your shoes or wipe them, because you want the dirt of the crossroads on your feet at all times.

When you arrive at the crossroads on the ninth night, you must face south, and soon you will see the Gray Man walking toward you. His skin is gray, his clothes are gray, his teeth are black. When he arrives before you, make your request. If it is money you want, he will spit out a coin that you must bury deep and water with tears. If it is love you want, he will whisper in your ear what you must do to ensnare your beloved. If it is skill you want, he will hand you a secret teaching.

After this you will see him only one other time—on the day you die. That is when he will turn up to collect what he is owed.

MEETING THE SERPENT

If there comes a time when you are so vexed at a person that you cannot see straight and your thinking has become all twisted up inside, you may want to seek out the Serpent and set him on the person. Steal from this vexing person a pair of shoes. Wait until there have been no storms, no rain, and no disturbance of the weather for sixteen days. Find a body of water with no stream and no creek letting out of it, and sink into it a bag of flour, a pound of pork, and a bottle of whiskey. Come back that night and wade into the water until you are neck-deep. Stand still, and after a time you will feel something sliding around your feet. The Serpent will rise up, and you will throw the shoes of the vexing person at him. He will swallow them, and you should leave without looking back.

Keep an eye on the vexing person. Eventually you will notice changes. The Serpent will slide into this person through his dreams and get into his skull. Once there, the Serpent will coil and twine inside his skin, and the vexing person will become full of distress as he feels the Serpent moving through his bones. He will tear at his hair and clothes and weep for many days, and the Serpent will only rest when the person has died, either at his own hand or at the hand of another. Meeting the Serpent is a serious matter and should be done with only the most vexing of individuals. Make sure that you truly cannot stand the person for one minute longer before setting the Serpent upon him.

DUPPIES AND BACKWARD-FACING MEN

Through this world wander many duppies, sick with grief, their heads twisted backward so they are always viewing the life they left behind. Duppies appear when loss is sharpest—

when a mother is about to lose a child, a father about to lose a son, a husband about to lose a wife. They smell the bitter stink of loss and they flock to it, like dogs creeping close to the fire, hoping to warm their cold bones with the pain of another. When death is on a house, you will see the hoot owl in the trees, peering in the window and looking down the chimney, before it flies away to summon the duppies. You can hear their weeping through the trees as they approach, and they surround a house all night, waiting for another lonely soul to join their number. But there is no pleasure in duppy companionship, no happiness in their company, and each lost soul in the mass of duppies feels as lonely as it did before.

To keep a body's soul from joining the ranks of the duppies and backward-facing men, you must tie the person's big toe to the bed with a white thread. Place three unhusked ears of corn underneath the mattress, and burn cherry root and oak bark in the room. If the person is showing distress, have her chew some alligator root to ease the restlessness. It is only a restless body that sends its soul out to the duppies. Keep the family close, and don't leave the person alone the entire night. When the sun rises, the family may rest but must maintain the vigil every night until the person has passed and for twelve hours afterward. Only a lonely soul can be pulled into the company of duppies, and so the body must be kept surrounded by family until the duppies slink back to their solitary burrows and bolt-holes.

Where stories bloom.

poppy

Visit us online at
www.pickapoppy.com